I0565698

SOMETHING FOUND

BOOK THREE ~ FUNERALS AND WEDDINGS SERIES

BERNADETTE MARIE

5 PRINCE PUBLISHING

Copyright © 2021 by Bernadette Marie, SOMETHING FOUND

All rights reserved.

This is a fictional work. The names, characters, incidents, and locations are solely the concepts and products of the author's imagination, or are used to create a fictitious story and should not be construed as real. No part of this book may be reproduced in any form or by any electronic or mechanical means, including information storage and retrieval systems, without written permission from the author, except for the use of brief quotations in a book review.

Published by 5 PRINCE PUBLISHING & BOOKS, LLC

PO Box 865, Arvada, CO 80001

www.5PrinceBooks.com

ISBN digital: 978-1-63112-268-2

ISBN print: 978-1-63112-269-9

Cover Credit: Marianne Nowicki

To Stan,

I'm blessed to have found you, and given the chance, I'd choose you again, and again, and again.

ACKNOWLEDGMENTS

To my boys: I found true happiness in being your mother. Thank you all for being amazing.

To my mom and sissy: I found that we are a unique trio and I cherish the fact that we still get to do everything together.

To Cate: I have found that I thrive under your guidance, as a person and an author. I also miss your face.

To my Book Hive and Street Team: I have found that your love and support is intoxicating. Thank you for showering me with it, and for volunteering to make my books look their very best.

To my Readers: I have found that I love writing stories that you love to read. Thank you for returning each time I put out a book, and for your kind words.

SOMETHING FOUND

*P*iles of plans and blueprints covered the top of Ray's desk. It was the season to plan out new builds which would begin in the spring. He'd picked up the contract on new multi-story condos, a city park, and a medical building.

He lifted his head when he saw Catherine walk from her office to the break room, no doubt for another cup of coffee. Life with an infant wasn't easy, he remembered.

Catherine's daughter was now six months old, but Catherine had only recently become her mother. Had she given birth to her, she'd have been prepared for sleepless nights. As it was, Celia Rose was an unexpected gift.

Ray swiveled his chair toward his computer to begin an email when Catherine walked into his office with two mugs of coffee.

"I thought you might want one," she said as she handed him one of the mugs and set down an orange wrapped piece of candy.

"Thank you." He took the coffee from her and the piece of candy, which Catherine had brought in to the office in an attempt to rid herself of extra Halloween candy at home. "Long night?"

"Celia Rose is trying to get her first tooth," she said as she yawned. "Alex had an early meeting, so I took night duty last night."

He remembered when he and his ex-wife would share the baby duties at night. That seemed so long ago now.

"I know this sounds like the standard response, but enjoy it. It goes so fast."

Catherine sipped her coffee. "I'm trying to absorb everything. Not getting to be part of her first five months, I want to remember all of it. It'll be different when we have more kids and I'm part of their creation process. But I want to be able to tell her everything."

"I assume you'll be at the YMCA on Sunday for basketball?"

"Yeah. Alex really missed those few weeks. He's been glad to get back to it. And I think that Celia Rose is ready for that kind of commotion," she smiled wide as she spoke of her daughter.

"I have the kids this week, and I know Charlotte is dying to see her again."

"Then I'll make sure we're there," she agreed as Allen at the front desk called to her to inform her that she had a phone call. "I guess my coffee break is over."

Ray watched as she walked back to her office. He was happy for Catherine and Alex. A new marriage and a new baby, it brought back a lot of memories.

He and Kelly had been divorced for two years, but they were amicable. He might even venture to say they were better friends than they had been before they got married.

They shared the kids and the responsibilities, only he lived in a different house, and not the one he'd bought.

Not everything turned out the way things were planned.

He sipped the coffee Catherine had handed him, and looked at the clock. It was ten-thirty. If he planned on getting through that stack on his desk in the next four hours, he needed to make a move. Kelly would bring the kids to the office after school.

It was a good thing they were amicable, because on his weeks with the kids, he saw his ex-wife every day when she'd drop them off after school.

Allen poked his head through the office door. "Kelly is on line one," he said.

Ray chuckled and looked at his watch. Day one of his week with the kids always started with the call during Kelly's planning period at school to make sure he knew what he was doing.

He'd been parenting their kids as long as she had, but Kelly always had an organization to her that led her to making him feel inferior. He wasn't going to forget things. He wasn't going to miss a step. But, he was about to take his bi-weekly phone call that assured that.

"Hey, Kel, what's up?" he said as he answered the phone.

On the other end of the line, he heard the familiar sigh since he'd shortened her name. It only started bothering her since they'd been divorced, but he couldn't help himself.

"Got ten minutes?"

"Ten? This usually takes five," Ray confirmed.

"Ray, just hear me out."

He leaned back in his chair and closed his eyes. "Go on."

"Charlotte had a cough this morning. It went away before school, but if it gets worse she'll have to stay home. Do you have Dr. Goodman's phone number?"

"Same doctor she's had since she was born?"

"Yes."

"Then, yeah, I have it."

"Don't let her around the baby if she's coughing." Wasn't that a given? "And call me if—"

"I got it," he bit out. "Continue."

He heard the inhale of frustration. "Connor is supposed to bring a treat to share on Friday that he made following a recipe. Now, I can keep him on Thursday and—"

"I can follow a recipe, Kel. What's next?"

"My mother's birthday—"

"Is on Wednesday. The kids will video call her on Wednesday night at six, does that work?"

"Ray…"

"I told you. I got this," he said as he sat up and put his feet on the ground. "You act like I don't know how to handle my own kids. We have this down, and have for two years. You let me see them on your weeks, and you see them at school, so you can check up on them. You and I can share a meal without a fight, and the kids are well adjusted. These phone calls of yours could be summed up in an email with dates, or you can tell me when you drop them off, and I'll handle it."

She was silent for a moment. "Fine. I don't mean to bother you when I call you."

Ray let out a breath. It was never a bother, and he shouldn't have responded like that. "I'm sorry. I'm going over contracts and budgets. Maybe I'm a little testy. What else?"

"Full day kindergarten has Connor exhausted." Which he already knew, but no more arguments, he promised himself. "Just make sure he's getting a good dinner and to bed on time. He has his Switch in his backpack, so take it away before bed. I don't know if he'll tell you he has it."

"Understood."

"I think that's it," she said, but Ray wasn't sure it was.

"Are you sure? And I'm not asking to be crappy, I'm asking because you sound preoccupied with another thought."

There was an uncomfortable pause. "Jeremy Cross asked me to dinner," she said, and the name socked Ray right in the gut.

"Oh, yeah? He'd asked about you the last time I saw him." Of course he did. He'd asked if his hot wife of his was still around, and it looked like he jumped on the news that they were divorced.

"His kids go to my school. I took his invite."

4

Ray winced. "I hope he takes you somewhere nice. What else do I need to know?"

"That's it. I'll have the kids to you by three."

"I can't wait."

CHAPTER 2

*K*elly collected the papers from each of her students. Fifth graders were unique, she thought as she walked past each of the kids while they put items back in their desks. They were a wonderful mix of little kid and big kid. Not yet a tween or even a teenager, they certainly weren't little anymore. Some knew too much about the world, and others had stuffed animals hidden in the bottoms of their backpacks. Some were already developing, others would be tiny for the next six years.

The demographics of the school had drastically changed over the past five years that she'd taught there. They had students who were growing up in multi-generational homes, one or two were homeless, and others lived in half-million dollar condos. What she loved about her classroom was the diversity, and she strove to mix that diversity together as much as possible. Oh, racism had snuck its evil head into her classroom of ten-year-olds more than once, but on any given day, every kid loved every other kid. That's what she'd wanted from her teaching experience. That's what true education was, she thought.

"Does everyone have everything put away?" she asked, and

there were various ways to say *yes* happening throughout the room. "Let's get our backpacks from our hooks and line up at the door."

At this point of the day, she would turn off the light, and it seemed to calm the students before they ran out the door.

When the bell rang, she opened the door, and as each student passed they would get a high-five.

"Goodbye, Mrs. Stewart," they would call and she would smile.

It had been a hard decision to keep her last name after the divorce, but it matched her kids' name. Only the Mrs. got her once in a while. Had she taken back her maiden name, Grady, then it would have sounded like they were talking to her mother.

When the inside door to the classroom opened, she saw the smiling faces of her own children as they ran to her and hugged her.

"Mama, I made you this," Charlotte handed her a drawing of a stick figure family, which always included their father.

"It's lovely," she said kissing the top of Charlotte's head. "Will you put it on my board?"

Charlotte nodded and headed to the small cork board where Kelly had designated a corner of it for Charlotte's art. She watched as her overly smart preschooler took down the artwork from the week before, put it in the basket on the counter, and added the new piece.

Connor plopped down in a chair at the reading table, and laid his head down on his folded arms. Kindergarten was taxing, Kelly thought.

She looked outside, making sure all of her students had made it to the pickup area, and then she closed the door and walked over to her son.

Pulling out a chair, she sat down next to him and rested her hand on his back. "Did the day wear you out?"

"Patrick doesn't have to go to school all day long," he said, mentioning the neighbor boy, his voice muffled against his arms.

"You're lucky to go to school all day. And Charlotte is too."

"Whatever."

She rubbed her hand down his back. "Let's get our stuff. Dad is waiting for you."

Charlotte hurried over to her, coughing as she did so. "Is the baby going to be there?"

"I doubt it. Catherine doesn't take her to work with her. And if you're coughing, I told Daddy not to let you around the baby. We don't want her to get sick."

Charlotte held her lips pursed as she coughed again. "I'm fine."

The colder weather was coming in, and Kelly wasn't worried that Charlotte would be sick, but it was a lesson in life as well.

WITH THE KIDS LOADED INTO THE MINIVAN, KELLY DROVE TOWARD Ray's office. Connor had fallen asleep the moment they'd turned out of the school's lot, and Charlotte bobbed her head to the songs on the movie she watched with her big pink headphones on.

Kelly was glad she got to see them every day, even on Ray's weeks. It was a perk to them going to the same school she taught at. Summers were different, she didn't see them all week when they were with him, but for nine months of the year they were still together—a family, she thought and then shook the thought away.

Of course they were a family. They'd always be a family. And the reason they lived apart was because when they did live under the same roof all she and Ray did was fight. This was a good arrangement. Perhaps Ray was the only one that lost out, she cringed. The kids saw her all the time, and him every other week.

Well, they wouldn't be the only kids that were raised in multiple homes. It was the norm. At least they saw him that often. When she was growing up, dads saw their kids on the weekends, or every other weekend. With this arrangement Ray was an active parent and had the kids just as much as she did.

When she pulled into the lot, the front door to the building opened, and Ray stepped out. It was his ritual. He worked hard to be present, and she had to give him credit for that.

Kelly parked the van, and within moments, Charlotte had unbuckled herself, opened the sliding door, and darted into her father's arms. He swung her around and kissed her cheeks.

"I've missed you, pretty girl," Kelly heard him say as he propped Charlotte on his hip.

Kelly climbed out of the van and walked to the other side, opening the door. "Hey, kiddo. We're here," she said as she ran a hand over Connor's hair.

"Hey, slugger," Ray's voice came softly from behind her, and she sucked in a breath as he set Charlotte down. "I'll carry him in."

Kelly unbuckled his seatbelt, and Ray hoisted him out of the car and started for the office. Taking another moment to collect herself, and the kids' items, Kelly took a few deep breaths.

It always stirred her up when she saw him with their kids. He was a good and attentive father. He'd been a good and attentive husband too. There had been a lot of stress in his life as money was tight and he was building his business, and in hers as she'd finished her grad school and tried to grow her family. The timing for everything had just been off, and it had cost them their marriage.

Everything had a purpose, including divorce.

CHAPTER 3

$\mathcal{K}$elly closed up the van and carried the kids' backpacks into the office. Catherine was already seated at the small table in the reception area with Charlotte coloring a picture.

"Hey, Kelly," she said as she smiled up at her. "Looks like Connor had a long day."

Kelly looked toward Ray's office where she saw he'd deposited Connor in the oversized chair, still asleep.

"He tells me full day kindergarten is hard."

Catherine picked up a new crayon. "I'm sure it is."

"Mom," Charlotte said, still coloring. "You can go. We're good."

The innocent words brought instant tears to Kelly's eyes, but she batted them away. "Okay. Let me kiss your brother goodbye."

Still carrying the backpacks, she walked to Ray's office, set down the backpacks, and kissed her son on the top of the head. He stirred and wearily opened an eye.

"I love you," she said. "Be good."

He nodded and went back to sleep.

As she turned to walk out of the office, she ran right into Ray, whom she hadn't heard walk in. He steadied her with his hand on her hips, and her hands came to his chest.

"Easy there," he teased as he stepped back. "Allen bought some of those Starbucks drinks you like in the bottles if you want to take one to go."

"I'm good. Headed to Zumba, so…"

"Good. You need to do something for yourself. Zumba and a dinner date."

She shook her head when he mentioned it. "Ray, don't go there."

"I'm happy for you. You should date. You're a beautiful, wonderful woman." But she heard the strain in his voice.

"Well, let's not mention it around the kids," she whispered. "I didn't discuss it with them."

Kelly walked past him and out to the reception area where she kissed Charlotte on the top of the head.

"Catherine, how's your daughter?" Kelly asked.

"Getting her first tooth. Instant parenthood did not prepare me for all of this, but I love her so much, it's worth it."

"That's wonderful. She's a blessing."

"She is that."

Kelly put her hand on Charlotte's head. "This one has a little cough. I told her not to be around the baby if she coughs."

Catherine nodded her head. "I'm sure we'll find some play-time when everyone feels perfect. Have a good night," she said, and Kelly took that as her exit.

She looked back at Connor, and Ray had taken a phone call. She let herself out of the office and walked back to the van.

Then, the tears streamed.

She wiped them away as she climbed into the van, and started the engine. She cried every time she dropped them off, and it wasn't as if she wouldn't see them all week, or as if this hadn't been the process for the past two years. But she couldn't help it.

Just as she put the van in reverse, the front door of the office opened, and Ray waved her back. No, she didn't want him to see her like this, but he was hurrying toward her.

Quickly, she put on her sunglasses and rolled down the window.

He lifted a bag and handed it to her. "Allen says he bought those drinks specifically for you, so you should take them."

"Thanks," she said, taking the bag and setting it on the seat.

"What's up? Are you crying?"

"Ray, I have to go. I'm fine."

"Put it in park, Kel," he demanded softly and she did so as he opened the car door. "What's wrong?"

"Nothing."

"Right. Nothing warrants tears."

"It happens every time I drop them off."

"You'll see them in the morning at school."

"I know. I can't help it."

He was smiling. God, she loved that smile. "I cry when I drop them off too. But I don't see them for a week."

"I know. This is petty."

"Unbuckle your seatbelt," he said, and he guided her from the van as she did so.

When her feet hit the ground, Ray gathered her in his arms and held her. It should have repulsed her and sent her into a fit of rage, but it didn't. There had always been a calm to his hugs. And even now, after two years without the man, it still brought calm.

When her breath returned to normal, he eased back. With the palm of his hand, he wiped away her tears.

"It's all okay," he said.

"I know."

And then he pressed a gentle kiss to her lips before he pulled back. Then he distanced himself. "I'm sorry. Old habits. Really old habits," he stammered as he ran his hands over his hair and then tucked them into his pockets. "I'll see you tomorrow. They're in good hands."

Kelly stood there, and watched as Ray disappeared back into the office. Pressing her fingers to her lips, her entire body trembled.

What was that, she wondered?

The tears were gone now, but her hands shook, and her breath came in short bursts.

It was a friendly gesture, only between them, it just confused things.

It was nothing.

Kelly climbed back in the van and threw it into reverse. She needed to get to Zumba and sweat out the anxiety that was building up inside of her.

Her kids were in good hands with their loving father and she had the night free. She needed to enjoy the benefits of being divorced and sharing custody.

Perhaps she'd call up her friends and share a bottle of wine. And having a blue and confusing day was just the reason to do so.

CHAPTER 4

*S*cents of dinner cooking on the stove and the sound of kids running through the house filled Ray's heart. He loved his weeks with his kids. It made him whole again.

When his phone buzzed in his pocket, he pulled it out to see his reminder to FaceTime his ex-mother-in-law. He thought it was interesting that Kelly hadn't called to remind him. She'd been quiet since she'd dropped the kids off on Monday and had cried in his arms.

Even today, when she'd dropped them off after school, she hadn't come into his office.

Perhaps that's how it should have always been, he thought as he turned off the heat on the stove and moved the pan to a cool burner.

"Hey guys, come in the kitchen please," he hollered over the television and the chatter in the other room.

A moment later, his son and daughter raced into the kitchen.

"Sit down at the table," he said as he picked up his iPad off the counter and set it on the kitchen table. "It's Grandma's birthday. Let's call her."

The kids situated themselves at the table and pushed their chairs together.

Ray scrolled through the contacts and clicked on Kelly's mother's. The screen popped up, and that horrible ringing sound of a FaceTime call filled the silence. A moment later, his ex-mother-in-law's face popped up on the screen and the kids began to talk at the same time.

As the kids talked to their grandmother, who was talking to them from her porch, which overlooked the beach, Ray went back to finishing dinner.

He listened as Charlotte told her grandmother about the petting farm that had come to school, and how she made jewelry out of macaroni that she had painted.

Connor talked about the boys in his kindergarten class who were playing baseball. He was very knowledgeable about them starting at T-ball and graduating out of that in first grade. Somewhere, Ray heard Connor mention that he thought Ray would be coaching.

Well, that was news to him. Perhaps he'd better brush up on his baseball. He was a basketball player. Leave it to his son to want to play something he didn't know as well.

Ray chuckled to himself. Maybe that's how his father had felt too. His father was a baseball player, and Ray wouldn't have anything to do with it. He'd played basketball from as far back as he could remember, through the competitive years, and on a full ride scholarship through college too. Now he played on Sundays with his teammates from college. It would be a good time to offer some bonding between his son and his father, he'd have to call and talk to him about it.

"Hello, Ray," he heard the voice of his ex-mother-in-law say.

When he turned back around, he noticed that his kids had fled, leaving their grandmother to watch him cook dinner.

"Hey, Ronda, happy birthday," he said as he took the seat his daughter had occupied.

"Thank you, sweetheart. How have you been? I haven't talked to you in a very long time."

"I'm good. Business is good. Kids are good."

Ronda smiled. "I'm happy for you. Kelly said you'd been doing well and playing basketball on the weekends."

He chuckled. Perhaps that weekly game was a bigger deal than he'd thought it was. "Yes. The guys I played with in college all meet each week for a game."

"Connor told me he likes those days."

And that squeezed at his heart. It was good for his son to see men bonding and enjoying time together. "I'm glad to hear he enjoys that. They're good men."

"Thank you for having them call me. It made my day."

"Happy birthday. Enjoy the rest of your evening."

They said their goodbyes and Ray turned off the iPad and set it back on the counter.

His in-laws had always been gracious to him, even through the hard times and when he and Kelly were headed toward divorce. Perhaps they had always known he and Kelly weren't right for one another. Perhaps it was a relief.

No, he didn't really believe that. No one wanted marriages to end. But the truth of the matter was, they did. Money was always an issue. Exhaustion from raising kids, furthering education, and building a business ultimately became too much, and even counseling didn't stop the inevitable.

Ray's thoughts were shifted as the kids ran through the kitchen and back out again, laughing. That was all that mattered to him. His children were happy and loved.

After dinner, they settled in to read a book before bed. Connor had chosen Harry Potter, and for the moment, Charlotte was content with that. He assumed when she found out how long a book it was, or how many books there were, she'd grow quickly tired of the story.

She'd seen the movies, but a book always transported the reader, or the listener, differently.

When Charlotte had dozed off, Ray carried her to bed. He then went to Connor's room to tuck him in.

"Tell me your Switch isn't under your pillow," Ray said and Connor rolled his eyes before pulling the game out from under his pillow as his father had said, and handing it to Ray. "Sneaky," Ray laughed.

He pulled up the blankets on Connor's bed, and kissed him on the forehead.

"I love you, kiddo."

"I love you too, Dad."

Ray walked toward the door and turned off the lights. But as he shut the door, he heard Connor call him back.

"What's up?"

"Is mom going to marry that other guy?"

The question had Ray frozen with his hand still on the door knob. "What other guy?"

"Sammy and Sophie's dad."

And Jeremy Cross was now part of the conversations he was having with his kids. He didn't like the man. He wasn't fond of his kids either, but Ray was man enough not to blame them for their shortcomings.

Ray walked over to the bed. "I don't think that's in her plans. She said their dad asked her to dinner. That's all."

"But that means they'll get married and have babies."

Ray tried to remember that a six-year-old's take on life was drastically different than a man's. But even hearing him say those words had Ray anxious too.

"I think they just want to have a meal together. I don't think they'll get married and have babies." He kissed his son's head again. "Okay?"

Connor nodded and Ray moved back to the door.

"Daddy," he called again and Ray stopped. "You and Mommy could get married again and have more babies. That would be okay."

And for a moment the air stuck in Ray's lungs. "Good night."

CHAPTER 5

The restaurant was busier than Kelly would have thought for a Thursday night. Her stomach twisted with nerves, and her mind kept going to her kids and what they'd think about her on a date.

She watched couples and families walk past her as she sat waiting for Jeremy to arrive. They'd agreed to meet at six, but it was inching toward six-thirty. Perhaps she'd been stood up.

Allowing him some grace, she'd give him ten more minutes and then she'd leave.

At eight minutes, she stood to leave when he walked in the door casually.

"Oh, good. You made it," he said as if he'd been waiting nearly forty minutes for her.

"I've been here for a bit," she said sweetly. "You did say six right?"

"Yeah, but the ex was on my phone, blabbering," he mimicked with his hand.

It had been years since she had been around the man, Kelly thought. They had dated briefly in college, before she'd met Ray, and then again when she and Ray had broken up for a few months.

Perhaps he felt comfortable with her, enough to sass about the ex-wife. She'd assume that was it, and that he wasn't being the ass it appeared he was being.

Jeremy walked to the hostess, winked, and asked for a table for two. Then, as the hostess led them to their table, he put his hand low on Kelly's back.

The intimate gesture sent a jolt through her. It had been nearly a decade since this man had touched her, and it had been two years since anyone had touched her.

Was she now so hard up for affection that she was accepting dates and reeling in the feelings of physical contact, no matter how minute they were?

When they reached their table, she sat down on one side of the booth, and she expected Jeremy to sit on the other side. Instead he sat down next to her, causing her to scoot over to make room.

"More intimate," he said as he winked at her.

Those dark eyes that once captivated her were now lined from age and sun. He was an avid golfer, and had a permanent sunny glow. She found, that despite his lateness, and his mocking of the ex, she was still drawn to his handsome face.

"I come here all the time. The chef knows me. Do you mind if I order?"

Kelly shrugged. "That would be fine."

"Okay, I'll go talk to him. I'll be right back."

The server returned to the table with a bottle of wine and two glasses. "The gentleman asked me to bring this while he's in the kitchen," she said as she poured the wine into the two glasses, and left the bottle.

Kelly thanked her, and sipped her wine. She looked around the restaurant at couples and parties enjoying their meals and conversations. She blew out a breath as she eased back in the booth, sipping her wine.

Her glass was empty when Jeremy finally returned to the table. "Sorry that took so long. We had a lot to catch up on," he said as he sat down and took a long drink from his wine. "So Sophie is hoping you'll be her teacher next year. It seems as if you're a favorite among the fourth grade class looking forward."

"That's nice to hear. It makes it worth it."

Jeremy slipped his arm around Kelly's shoulders. "This is nice," he said as he sipped his wine. "We were good together, remember?"

"That was a very long time ago." And she didn't remember them being so good together.

"Well, it'll be nice to spend some time together." Jeremy took a long drink from his glass. "How long have you and Ray been divorced?"

"Two years."

"Six for us," he pushed away his glass. "As soon as the kids were here, we just couldn't make it work."

Kelly felt her shoulders ease under his arm. "Same. It was exactly what we wanted, a family. And then it fell apart. I was going to grad school, he was building a business. Money was tight." She took a breath and realized she was emotionally dumping a lot of personal information. "Sorry."

Jeremy filled her glass from the bottle and topped his off. "Don't be sorry. This is what divorced people talk about. I've been on seven dates in six years, and it usually starts like this."

"Sad."

"Very sad," he said sincerely. "But, you and I have a history, so it actually feels like talking to an old friend."

And suddenly, he didn't seem so creepy to her as he slid her glass to her, and lifted his for a toast.

Kelly did the same.

"To old friends who fell down the same well. May we find recovery together."

She tapped her glass to his and they both sipped. Perhaps the night was salvageable after all.

The server brought out three different plates of food and two empty plates. Jeremy thanked her, and finally removed his arm from Kelly's shoulders.

"Do you remember that lake we used to go to in college?"

Instantly she felt her cheeks fill with heat. "I remember it." Or she remembered the nights in the back of his truck, under the stars.

"You were the first girl I ever took up there," he admitted as he began to dish food onto each of the empty plates.

"Liar. I don't believe you."

"It's true. Until I met you, I'd only had one other girlfriend, in high school."

"I never knew that."

"I have to admit. When we broke up, and you met Ray, I was devastated. Then we got back together, but you went back to Ray. I knew then it was a lost cause for us. Now here we are."

"We're just having dinner."

"Of course, but it's admittedly an interesting change of events."

Was it, she wondered? Oh, the man had always captivated her and enraged her all at the same time. When she'd found out that his kids went to the same school she taught at, that had sent her into an emotional spin for sure. Ray had had the same reaction. Though he was cordial to Jeremy, he certainly didn't like him, for good reason.

Well, she reminded herself, Ray didn't have a say in whom she saw. No, as friendly as they were, and as well as they co-parented, he didn't get a say.

Jeremy filled his fork from his plate and held it in front of

Kelly's mouth. "You're going to love this," he said, as she opened her mouth and took the bite he offered.

As she chewed, she thought of new beginnings—or reconnections as the case might be, and decided she was ready for them.

CHAPTER 6

elly moved about her classroom an hour before school started. She had her cup of coffee and her muffin on her desk. She had graded the assignments she'd neglected to grade over the weekend, and had written the agenda on the white board.

When her classroom door opened, she looked up at the clock. There were fifteen minutes before school opened to the kids, but her children ran through the door.

Kneeling down, she scooped them into her arms and placed noisy kisses all over their faces.

"I missed you," she said, as she looked at their tired faces.

"Mommy, I got to hold the baby," Charlotte said enthusiastically.

"You did? What a big girl."

"She smiled at me too."

"Of course she did," Kelly said before kissing the top of her daughter's head. "And you, sleepy face? What did you do?" she asked her son.

"I shot hoops with the guys. Craig lifted me up so I could hang from the basket."

Kelly pressed her hand to her chest. "That's pretty high."

"He stood there until I was ready to drop."

"He's a nice guy."

When she looked up at the door, Ray stood there casually leaned up against the doorjamb. He smiled at her with that smile that still did her in.

She stood and took her children's hands. "I suppose we'd better get you two to class."

As they walked toward the door, Ray stood up straight. "I'll walk with you. Then can we talk for two minutes?"

Kelly looked up at the clock. "It's going to be tight. Can I call you later, or..."

"Only two minutes, Kel."

She nodded, and as a family they walked down the hall to the kindergarten room, where Connor walked through the classroom and then out the door to stand with his class.

They then walked down to the other end of the school and outside to the adjacent building where the preschool and daycare was held. They kissed Charlotte goodbye and watched as she ran off independently to play in the small house on the playground with her friends.

"Okay, we have a two minute walk back," Kelly said as she wrapped her arms around herself to shield from the November cold as they walked back to the main building.

"Connor has some concerns," Ray began.

"About what?"

"You getting married to Sammy and Sophie's dad."

Kelly stopped and turned to look up at Ray. "You told him I went out with him?"

"I didn't have to. Kids talk too."

"I'm not going to run off and marry Jeremy."

Ray shrugged. "I'm filling you in. He's concerned that you're going to marry him and make more babies."

Kelly shook her head as she began walking again. "I'm a grown woman. I can do what I want."

"I'm not arguing that. I'm letting you know that your son has concerns and he also says we could have more babies, that would be okay."

"We?"

"You and me."

Kelly let out a breath. "That's a lot of information for a Monday morning."

"We share this kind of stuff, right? That's what makes this co-parenting thing work."

He was right, but now she needed to decide how she was going to handle it. She'd gone to dinner with Jeremy on Thursday, and again on Saturday. The only difference was, when Jeremy dropped her off at home on Saturday, he'd kissed her goodbye, and that had sent off a lot of sparks.

Understandably, that was from the years she hadn't been kissing men, since she and Ray separated. But it had felt awfully nice.

"I'll head to work. I'm around all week if you or the kids need anything. Maybe we can all go for ice cream on Wednesday so I can see them."

"It's November, Ray."

He chuckled and that undid her too. "Happy Meals? Wednesday at five-thirty?"

She smiled at him and touched his arm. "We'll meet you there."

"Thanks. See you then," he said as he turned and walked down the hallway and disappeared.

RAY WALKED OUT TO HIS CAR, OPENED THE DOOR, AND SAT. THERE was no need to drive away for the next ten minutes. The line of minivans and SUVs filed in and out of the lot systematically.

He drank his coffee and thought about the brief conversation he'd had with Kelly. Connor wasn't a huge fan of Sammy and Sophie, and he assumed that some of his worry over Kelly and Jeremy getting married and having babies stemmed from that dislike. But Kelly was right, it wasn't anyone's business whom she dated, though Ray couldn't help but think she could do better. Hell, she'd already dated this guy multiple times, really, she should try something new.

Then again, Kelly liked to try and fix what was broken—usually. When he'd said the infamous words, *then why don't we just end it and get a divorce*, she hadn't done too much to fix that.

He sipped his coffee again, and then returned the cup to the cupholder.

The traffic was dying down, so he'd head to work.

As he maneuvered out of the school lot, he considered that maybe he was just jealous. He hadn't had a date in a year, and he hadn't told Kelly about the date he'd had, perhaps because it hadn't gone well.

This was part of divorce. The learning how to watch your "significant other" move on without you. The process might have been easier if they hadn't had kids, but then again, he couldn't deny that those kids were his entire life—and Kelly's too.

Ray would just have to deal with the fact that he was watching his wife—his ex-wife he reminded himself—move on from him. In college, they'd broken up and gotten back together. That's not how it worked in the real world.

As he pulled into the lot, he watched Catherine climb from her car and then pull Celia Rose from her car seat.

"Do you need some help?" he asked as he parked and opened his door.

"I'm so sorry to bring her. The sitter called in sick and Alex had a meeting. My mom will be here in an hour to pick her up."

Ray laughed. "Don't worry about it. Connor and Charlotte have had impromptu days here before, too." He walked to her and took the baby from her. "We'll head in and have a moment. I'm probably the only one who hasn't had some one on one time with this cutie."

CHAPTER 7

There were chores, groans, nudging, and more groans. Connor carried the dishes from the table, and Charlotte put away the condiments in the refrigerator.

Kelly watched as each minute chore was accomplished. When that was done, the kids came back to the table, and on her iPad, she called their father.

When it began to ring, she stepped away from the table and went about loading the dishwasher while the kids talked to their father as they did every evening when they were with her.

Connor quickly told him how he'd like to play baseball, again, and he'd promised, again, to look into it for the spring. Charlotte had a story about playing at school, and a book they read, and an art project with glitter.

Kelly laughed as she added dishes to the wash.

"Your turn, Mom," Connor yelled as they both ran out of the room.

She laughed as she walked back to the table and Ray was still there. "Sorry about that. I have to teach them how to say goodbye properly."

"Yeah, they did that to me the other night with your mom."

Kelly sat down in the chair Charlotte had occupied. "She was very happy you had them call. Thanks for that."

"She's their grandmother. She deserved to talk to her grand-kids, even if she's living on a beach," he teased and Kelly relaxed in the chair.

"Seriously, how spoiled could they be?" she laughed.

"They worked hard for that. Someday, maybe we'll be living on a beach too. Or on beaches," he corrected. "I'll let you get back to it. I'm headed over to Toby's for boys' night."

"Is that a thing?"

"Has been since Alex moved home. Catherine and Rachel have nachos and margaritas. We have beers and play pool."

"Rachel is pregnant, isn't she?"

"Yeah, it's been their tradition for a long time, the name just doesn't change."

"Got it. How is she? I mean…"

"After she got shot?"

Kelly let out a breath thinking of the school shooting where Rachel had been shot in the shoulder. "Yeah."

"She's good. She's seeing a therapist."

"She is a therapist."

"And they need them too. But, honestly, I think she's really healthy, mentally and physically. She has scars from her surgeries, but the baby is growing, and she's doing really well. I'm sure she'd love to see you."

"Oh, I don't know about that."

"Seriously. Maybe come by on a Sunday sometime when we're playing basketball. The kids love to be there."

"I'll think about it."

There was a moment of silence and Ray cleared his throat. "I'll let you go. Tell the kids I love them one more time."

"I will."

"And, Kel, sweet dreams," he said before disconnecting the call.

. . .

RAY CLOSED HIS IPAD AND SAT IN THE SILENCE OF HIS HOUSE. Maybe he should just stay home for the night and get some rest. He had some plan reviews to go over, and a few emails he could attend to.

No. Part of his week included the night at Toby's. He was just feeling bad for himself, as he did every night after he talked to his kids, but didn't tuck them in or kiss them before bed.

He wasn't the first parent to live though this. He wouldn't be the last.

As he readied himself to leave the house, his phone rang, and he answered it to hear his father's boisterous voice.

"Ray!"

Because it always made his father sound like a game show host, Ray laughed. "What's up, Dad?"

"Not much. What are you doing?"

"Headed to Toby's for a few beers."

"In that mansion?"

Ray grinned. "Yes. He has a game room in the basement. You should go with me someday."

"Really. I'd like that. Not tonight. I didn't ask permission two days ago," he teased, and Ray heard his mother's voice in the background scolding him.

"Okay. Get permission for next time."

"You bet. When do you have your kids? I have a lead on some Bronco tickets, and I want you and me to take Connor to a game."

"Dad, he'd love that."

"Charlotte and your mother can have a nice afternoon. We'll have a boys' day."

"He'll be here next Sunday."

"Okay," he heard his father mumble the dates. "I'll get them for that day."

"He will be very excited."

"Let him know. I'll let you go. You have fancy beer and pool to get to."

Ray laughed again. "I'll talk to you later, Dad. I love you."

"I love you too, son," he said and Ray heard his mother's voice again. "And your mother loves you too."

"I love her too, bye."

He disconnected the call and continued to smile. Did a boy ever stop thinking his dad was some kind of hero? His father certainly was one to Ray.

Growing up his dad had been larger than life. A fire captain, Ray could remember going to the station on field trips and all of the firemen knowing his name. It was a bigger than life kind of moment. His father was a big man, and add full bunker gear, the man was even bigger.

He remembered many nights being awaken by the sound of an alarm, and his father would run off to fight a fire. When he was in middle school, the department went from volunteer to paid, and his father then was gone twenty-four hours at a time.

George Stewart saved kids from burning houses and wrecked cars, but sometimes, he didn't get there fast enough. Though his saves outweighed the tragedies, those were the memories his father carried with him—that burdened him.

The fire department always offered their fighters therapy. His dad was wise enough to take it, and as far as Ray knew, even in retirement, he was part of a support group to help others get through the trauma they went through every day.

He was a good role model for Ray and his brother. Ray could only hope that as a grown man, Connor would someday think the same about him.

CHAPTER 8

*R*ay looked down at his watch, on Monday afternoon, when he heard tires on gravel. It was three-thirty, and he stood from his desk and hurried to the door.

Connor was already out of the minivan when Ray opened the front door to the office.

"Hey, big man!" Ray said as Connor ran up to him and hugged him tightly around the neck. "How was school?"

Connor held up a medal that hung around his neck. "I got an award."

"No kidding. What for?"

"Fastest runner in gym class. Someone wins it every week. I got it this week."

"Very nice," he set his son back on the ground as Charlotte ran toward him. He scooped her up, just as he had Connor. "Hello, my princess." He gave her a noisy kiss on the cheek.

"We got a new friend at school today. Her name is Maddison."

"And did you play with her?"

"Yep. She has a dog, and a cat, and three fish."

"That's a lot."

"Can we have a dog?"

He let out a hum. "That'll be a discussion for another day," he said as he set her down and watched as Kelly walked toward him carrying their backpacks.

"If you run, I'll scoop you up too," Ray teased and Kelly shook her head at him.

"We'd both be in chiropractic care after that."

"I could do it."

"No doubt," she agreed as she handed him the bags. "Connor has a birthday invitation in his backpack. It's during your week, so see if it works out. I'll let the mom know."

"Okay. Would you like to come in? Have something to drink and say bye to the kids?"

She looked past him into the office and shook her head. "I think they're all settled. I'll head out. I'll see you tomorrow," she said as she walked back to the van.

Ray watched her go, as he had hundreds of times before, and he would do again tomorrow. As she pulled away, he waved before walking back into the office.

As usual, Charlotte colored with Catherine, who was taking a coffee break, and Connor sat on Ray's oversized chair playing on his Switch.

"So I have a big surprise for you."

Connor looked up from the game, his eyes wide. "Really? Just for me?"

"Yeah." Ray sat down next to him. "Grandpa got Bronco tickets for Sunday. He's going to take us to the game."

"No way," his eyes had gone even wider. "Mitchell McCormick is going to be so jealous of me."

Ray laughed. "Your sister is going to have a girl day with Grandma. So it'll be just us guys."

Connor's face grew serious again. "Will we have to miss basketball?"

"No."

"Oh, good. Craig said he'd let me hang from the net again."

34

~

ZUMBA HAD KICKED KELLY'S ASS, SHE THOUGHT AS SHE FELL ONTO the couch with a bottle of water. It was good though. When the kids were with Ray, it kept her mind occupied. When Connor had FaceTimed her on Monday night, he'd been full of stories about getting to go to a Bronco game on Sunday, and apparently, while he was at the game, Charlotte was going to get to go to high tea at the Brown Palace.

There was a part of her that was immensely jealous. She wanted to go to Bronco games and high tea. She laughed. She knew full well her ex-mother-in-law would take her if she asked.

Tilting her head back against the couch, she closed her eyes. By Thursday nights Kelly was exhausted. The lack of routine she normally had when the kids were around made her lethargic, even though she'd worked out.

As she rested there, she heard a car pull up in front of the house, as if they'd parked in the driveway. Then she heard the car door close, and a moment later there was a knock on the front door.

Prying her eyes open, she slowly stood and walked to the door. It was past seven o'clock. She wasn't expecting anyone.

When she looked through the peephole she saw Jeremy standing on the doorstep. Had they had plans?

She opened the door and he leaned against the jamb like a cool drink of water. "I was hoping you were home," he said as he slid past her and into her house. "Were you working out?"

"Just got home."

"Zumba?"

"Yes."

"My ex-wife was into that for a long time. Now she's into yoga. I can't keep up. I thought I'd stop by and have a drink."

"Oh, I'm not sure what I have. I might have some wine," Kelly said as she walked toward the kitchen and he followed, which made her fully aware of how she looked.

She was still in her workout attire. Her hair was pulled up on top of her head, and sans any makeup. There was a chance she might smell too, but she wasn't going to worry about that.

Kelly opened the refrigerator and pulled out the bottle of wine she had there. Handing it to Jeremy, she took down two glasses and walked to the table, again he followed.

She pulled out the stopper and filled each of their glasses.

"We could sit in the living room," she offered, and realized he was gazing down at her.

"You are as beautiful as you were in college."

"Oh, I don't know about that."

His hand came to her cheek. "It's true," he said before dipping his head and kissing her. But he didn't ease back and read her expression. Instead, he moved in closer and deepened the kiss.

Kelly eased against him, letting her head swim with the kiss. It was familiar, it was nice. For an instant, she thought of how different it was than Ray's kisses—which she missed, but it was nice.

Jeremy pressed his forehead to hers as he pulled back from the kiss. "Let's go sit on the couch and enjoy this, and maybe just a little more of this," he said before kissing her again.

CHAPTER 9

The kids had gone with Ray to Toby's house, and had
fallen asleep on the ride home. Of course they had, he
thought as he shut the door to Connor's room after having
tucked him in.

They'd jumped on Toby's trampoline, played pool, sat in the
hot tub, and filled their bellies with pizza. Thursdays with his
boys was important to him, and it seemed to be equally as important to his children.

They had managed to stay awake just long enough for show-
ers, though he wasn't sure just how clean they got.

Ray walked through the house assuring all the doors were
locked. He looked through their backpacks making sure everything was tucked in it, or taken out of it. He'd cleaned out their
lunch boxes and added the dry items for the morning's lunch
packing. Now, he'd go to his room, turn on the TV and have a
grateful moment to himself.

The local news rounded up the important stories, and his eyes
began to close. He'd force them back open, but a few moments
later, his lids would grow heavy.

When his phone rang on the night stand, Ray jolted awake.

The news was over and some show he'd never seen before with a laugh track was playing.

He picked up his phone and saw his mother's name. "Mom? It's eleven o'clock. Is everything okay?"

Ray heard her sniff before he heard her take a breath to talk through her tears. "They're heading to the hospital."

"Who?" he asked as he sat up and began looking for the clothes he'd taken off.

He had his pants on before she said, "Your dad. He had a heart attack. They're taking him to the hospital."

Ray sat down on the bed to catch the breath that had suddenly been sucked from his lungs. He could now hear voices behind his mother, which he assumed belonged to paramedics. "What happened?"

"He woke up saying his chest hurt, and then…"

"Okay. Where are they taking him?"

"Saint Joe's."

"I'll be right there," Ray said as he pulled on his shirt.

"Don't wake the kids."

"I'll be there," he said before his mother hung up to ride in the ambulance.

KELLY WONDERED WHAT THE HELL SHE WAS DOING. SHE WAS FLAT on her back on the couch, Jeremy's body was heavy on top of hers, and they'd been making out like a pair of teenagers for hours.

Even as he ran kisses down her neck, she had to admit, she was surprised that he hadn't just assumed she'd have sex with him. He'd been very mindful of his hands and lips.

Just as he brought his mouth back to hers, her cell phone rang in the kitchen.

"Too bad for whoever that is," Jeremy said as she pushed her hands against his shoulders.

"That's Ray's ring."

"He's always been my buzz kill," Jeremy said, looking down at her.

"It's eleven o'clock. Something might be wrong."

Jeremy eased back off her and she crawled off the couch, and hurried to the kitchen. "Hello?"

"I need you," his voice came with a solid dose of panic.

"What happened? Connor? Charlotte? God, what did you let them do?"

"Your vote of confidence is amazing," he snapped. "My dad is on his way to the hospital. He had a heart attack or something. I need you to come here and be with the kids."

"I'm on my way."

Jeremy was standing behind her when she disconnected the call. "Something happened?"

"His dad had a heart attack. I have to go be with the kids."

"Get your stuff. I'll walk out with you."

Kelly's mind was jumbled. She needed clothes for the next morning, her bag, her keys, her charger—what if she forgot something? Did it even matter?

Jeremy stood by the door with it open when she ran back through the kitchen.

"I'm sorry," she said as she passed by him and he closed the door.

"Not for this you're not. Your family needs you."

And she felt her heart squeeze when he acknowledged them. Then the guilt for what she'd been doing balled in her gut.

~

RAY OPENED THE FRONT DOOR WHEN HE SAW THE HEADLIGHTS from Kelly's car in the driveway. His hands shook, so he tucked them in his pockets as he watched her hurry from her car.

"Go. I'm here," she said as she dropped her bag by the door, but he needed a moment, so he pulled her in to him tightly and held her.

Kelly's arms came around him without saying a word.

Ray buried his face into her shoulder and then he felt the tears. With Kelly, tears didn't matter. She'd never judge him for them, so he let them flow.

Her hand came to the back of his head and she held him there until he could breathe again.

"Thank you for coming over. They just got to the hospital."

"We'll be here, and I'll get them to school." Ray nodded and Kelly cupped his face in her hands. "Call me if you need me, and keep me updated."

Ray took her hands and held them in his. "Thank you."

KELLY WATCHED AS RAY HEADED OUT OF THE HOUSE TO HIS CAR, and stood in the doorway until he'd backed out of the driveway and had driven off.

Then her tears began. She closed the door and dropped to the floor. George Stewart was as much a father to her as her own. Her heart ached just thinking about him in pain. And Clara, what was she going through watching the man she loved suffer? When she realized just how loud she was sobbing, she covered her mouth. Their kids had a way of knowing when she was crying. They always found her in her bathroom or closet. She needed to pull it together before one of them ended up hearing her.

She also needed to get some sleep. Kelly stood and walked down the hallway. Stopping at the first door, she opened it to look in on Connor who slept soundly in his sports themed room. She closed the door and moved to the next, opening it and looking in. The night light cast pink stars on the ceiling of Charlotte's princess room.

Kelly smiled at her sweet girl, her arms wrapped around a well-loved teddy bear. She closed the door and turned around to the open door across the hallway. It was the only room she'd never been in in the house. When Ray had moved in, and the kids saw their new rooms, they'd wanted her to see them. But Ray's door had been shut. Now she stood there looking into the bedroom of a single man.

The light on the nightstand was on. The sheets had been crawled out of. It was painted in contrasting shades of gray, drawn blinds covered the window, and the TV on the dresser was bigger than the one in the living room. A bathroom was connected to the bedroom.

It reminded her that she hadn't showered since her Zumba class. Perhaps she'd shower, and it would be one less thing to think about in the morning.

She gathered her bag from the front door and headed to Ray's bathroom so she wouldn't wake up the kids as it neared midnight. As the shower warmed, she pulled a clean towel from under the sink. Because she had to, because being the ex dictated it, she opened the medicine cabinet.

Toothbrush, deodorant, Tylenol, multi-vitamin, and cologne. Without touching anything, she stood on her toes to look on the top shelf. Razor, razor blades, thermometer, and a tube of Neosporin.

She wasn't sure what she was looking for, but there was relief in the normality of the items, and maybe a little relief that there wasn't a box of condoms.

Discarding her workout clothes, she pulled the tie from her hair, and stepped into the water. She let the warmth envelop her as she tipped her head back into the water. Taking the shampoo, she lathered it into her hair, and soaped up with his body wash, and then the tears returned.

The scents that surrounded her were all too familiar, and the comfort of them caused her heart to ache for what they'd lost when they'd walked away from their marriage.

Her mind went to Ray sitting at the hospital, and the tears came harder.

Knowing he was emotionally in pain, and his family was suffering, her heart ached. She was nothing but an outsider now, and that hurt.

CHAPTER 10

*R*ay stood in the doorway of his bedroom and looked at Kelly sleeping in his bed. He wiped his eyes, which were weary and still welled with tears. The night he'd just endured had been the most horrific of his life. Seeing Kelly in his bed brought him comfort, and he was in serious need of comfort.

He toed off his shoes and walked to the bed before Kelly stirred, and then jolted awake.

"I didn't hear you come in," she said as she sat up. "What time is it?"

"Five."

"I'll move. I just fell asleep here. I should have slept on the couch, but…"

"Shhh," he said as he moved to the bed, and laid down next to her.

Kelly rolled to her side to face him, tucking her hands under her cheek. "How is your dad?"

The question had him reaching for her and gathering her up in his arms.

"Ray?" Her warm breath was soft against his cheek. "Tell me," she said, and he heard the tears in her voice before he felt them against his skin.

"He died," was all he could say before he broke down.

Kelly's arms wrapped around him, and she pulled him closer.

Ray clung to her like a child to his mother as he sobbed. Kelly's hands cradled the back of his neck as her tears soaked his shirt.

"I am so sorry," she said through her own sobs. "I loved him. I truly did," she said as she pressed a kiss to his temple.

"He loved you, too," Ray confirmed as he pulled her in even tighter.

They laid there like that until the tears ran dry, comforted in one another's arms. Then Kelly eased back.

"I should go call for a sub."

Ray searched her tear-streaked face in the subtle light of dawn. "Why?"

"I want to help you and your mother. You need to mourn. Someone else needs to help you so you can do that. I can help with arrangements, and make phone calls. I'll call and let Father Dawson know that…"

Ray pulled her back in and pressed a kiss to her lips, lingering there until she eased against him.

When he released her she sucked in a breath. "What was that for?"

"Comfort. You always have my back."

"Of course I do. I might not be your wife, but I am the mother of your children, and I am forever tied to your family."

She'd always be more than that to him, he thought. She was his first love, and he'd never get over that, even if someone else came along.

Kelly rolled from the bed and picked up her phone from the night stand. As she walked out of the room, Ray softly called after her.

She turned back to him.

"Make your call, then come back."

Worry lit in her eyes, but she nodded, then walked out of the room.

KELLY TOOK A MOMENT AFTER CALLING IN FOR A SUB AND excusing the kids from school. Ray would want their comfort too.

Tucking her phone into her bag by the door, she pressed her fingers to her lips. The kiss he'd planted on her still sizzled through her. The kisses that she'd shared with Jeremy hadn't had the same effect.

Crawling back in bed with him would be a mistake. They weren't married. They weren't involved. She could comfort him just as well from across the room, but the draw was great. She wanted to crawl into his bed and hold him.

He was snoring softly as she walked back into the bedroom. That was better, she thought. He'd never know if she didn't crawl back in.

Just as she turned to leave the bedroom, he called after her softly. "Please come lay down."

Kelly turned back, took a moment, and then walked toward the bed and slid in next to him. She rolled so her back was to him, and he moved in so that his arms came around her.

The familiar feelings washed over her, and comforted her like a blanket on a cold night. This would confuse things in the morning, she knew. Certainly she couldn't let the kids see them, it would confuse them too.

Again, Ray snored softly, and Kelly closed her eyes. This was comfortable to him, it eased his pain. For that reason, she could remain there in his arms for just a little bit.

. . .

"Mom. Mommy," the small voice stirred her. "Mommy, wake up."

Kelly's eyes shot open and Charlotte and Connor stood in front of her, their hands on her arm and Ray's arms wrapped around her.

"We're late. We didn't make it to school. You and daddy are sleeping," Charlotte said and Kelly realized she'd never set her alarm because she'd never gone to bed in her own bed.

Ray stirred behind her, lifted onto his elbow, and wiped his eyes. "What time is it?"

"Eight," Connor said.

"Okay," Ray laid back for a moment before sitting up. "The two of you go brush your teeth, get dressed, and meet me in the kitchen. I want to talk to you."

"About you and Mommy being married again?" Charlotte asked as Connor began pushing her out of the room. "What?" she argued with Connor. "They're sleeping in the same bed. Mommy is here," they heard her say as they walked down the hallway.

Ray wiped his hand over his face, and Kelly sat up. "I should have slept on the couch. They're going to be so confused."

"We weren't doing anything."

"They don't understand what that would mean anyway."

"What they're going to understand is we are friends. We were friends before we were married, and we remain friends after. When they know why you're here, they'll understand."

Kelly nodded in agreement. "I'll get my bag and get changed," she said before kicking her feet over the edge of the bed, but Ray pulled her back, and down on the bed.

She looked up at him as he lowered himself to her. "Maybe this would all be worth it if we'd just done this," he said before he lowered his mouth to her and kissed her. She didn't jerk away, but it took a moment to realize what he was doing.

Ray deepened the kiss and Kelly closed her eyes. What did she have to lose?

She wrapped her arms around his neck and let the moment swirl around her, as if she'd drank too much wine.

$\mathcal{K}$elly gathered her items from her bag, and walked to where she heard the commotion in the bathroom. Connor was helping, or bossing his sister to brush her teeth while she made faces in the mirror.

"C'mon, let's get our teeth brushed," Kelly said and they both stopped to look at her.

"Why are you here?" Connor asked.

"Daddy needed me to take care of you guys late last night."

"I didn't know you were here."

"No, you were asleep. Now brush your teeth." She stepped up to the sink and helped Charlotte get her toothbrush wet, and added toothpaste. Then she did her own. They had their normal morning routine, but this was just a different setting, she thought.

When they were done, she wiped off both of their faces with the hand towel, because she didn't know if he had wash cloths in his drawers, and didn't want to go looking. She took the brush she'd brought in for her hair, and ran it through both of theirs. Charlotte handed her the hair band she wanted her to use, and Kelly put Charlotte's hair into a ponytail.

"Now, go get dressed and meet Daddy at the table like he asked."

When they'd hurried off, Kelly turned on the water and splashed her face. The tears from the early morning cry with Ray showed in her eyes. She was pale, which came from lack of sleep, and her stomach twisted. They were about the tell their children that their beloved grandfather had died unexpectedly.

The very thought of it brought tears back to her eyes, so she shut the door and let herself cry it out. When she heard the kids run back down the hall, she finished up and headed to the kitchen.

Ray had bowls for cereal set out on the table for them, and a mug of coffee ready for her.

It all felt too familiar, but in the moment, perhaps that was the best thing.

"Why were you sleeping with Mommy?" Connor asked him, as if Kelly's answer hadn't sufficed.

She took the coffee Ray offered her and watched as he sat down at the table.

"I needed her here last night. I had to go somewhere," he said as he poured cereal into each of their bowls and then added milk.

He lifted his eyes to her as if he needed her strength closer to him, so Kelly pulled out another chair and sat down.

Ray sat down, his coffee mug between his hands. He looked at the kids and batted his eyes, she knew to ward off the tears. Then he reached for her hand.

"I called Mommy very late last night and asked her to come sit with you both." He blew out a steady breath. "Grandma called me last night and told me that Grandpa was very sick and the ambulance had come for him."

Connor took a bite of his cereal, then put his spoon down and drank from his milk. Charlotte had already begun to cry, but she didn't move from her seat.

"I had Mommy come over here and I went to be with Grandpa."

Connor stirred his spoon through his cereal. "He's still sick, huh? That's why you let us stay home from school?"

Ray squeezed Kelly's hand. "I needed you here with me today. See, Grandpa got very sick very fast." He blew out another breath as if to settle himself. "They took him to the hospital, but he didn't get better."

Charlotte hopped down from her chair and jumped up into Ray's lap. He let go of Kelly's hand and wrapped his arms around their daughter.

"It's okay, Charlotte," he whispered in her ear.

Connor pushed his bowl back. "What happened to him? We're going to the Bronco game on Sunday."

Kelly reached for Connor's hand, but he pulled back and rested it in his lap. She looked at Ray who held Charlotte to him.

"Well, kiddo," he spoke to Connor. "Grandpa was so sick, his heart stopped. He died last night."

Kelly heard Charlotte sob against Ray's shoulder and he rubbed her back as tears streamed down his cheeks.

Connor pushed himself away from the table and ran down the hall. A moment later his bedroom door slammed.

Kelly stood from the table, and Ray touched her arm. "Let him have a moment."

She sat back down, Ray's hand still on her arm, and their daughter still wrapped around him.

RAY HELD CHARLOTTE A BIT LONGER BEFORE HANDING HER TO Kelly and walking down the hallway to Connor's bedroom.

He knocked softly, and then entered the room to find his son sitting in the beanbag in the corner, a baseball in his hands.

Connor looked away from him as he sat down on the bed. "You doing okay?"

Connor didn't answer.

"It's okay to be mad. It's okay to be sad and to cry. Grandpa was very important to us all."

The ball shifted from hand to hand, but still he said nothing.

"We're going to spend the day as a family. In a little while, we're going to go over to Grandma's and be with her too. She's very sad, and there are lots of plans to make. Mom is going to go with us."

Connor pulled the ball to his chest. "I didn't know Mom was here last night."

"You were both asleep. I didn't know when I'd get home."

"Why can't we all just live in the same house?"

"Because your mom and I aren't married anymore."

"Why?"

Ray had to take a moment. Connor would have only been four when they separated, and at that time there was some excitement to having two bedrooms. But his kids were smarter that Ray ever gave them credit for.

"Sometimes things just don't work out, kiddo. Mommy and I didn't get along anymore. She was going to school. I was building a business. We argued all the time. It was better for us to be apart."

"I don't think so."

Ray moved from the bed to sit on the floor next to his son. "Mommy will always be one of my best friends."

"Like Uncle Craig?"

"Exactly. Your mom and I were friends before we got married, and now we're friends again."

"And friends have sleepovers like you and Mommy?"

Ray puffed up his cheeks and let the air out slow. "I needed some comfort last night. I asked Mommy to stay there with me so I could hold her. Like a comfy teddy bear."

Connor considered that. "Because you're friends?"

"Because we're friends."

51

"I'm going to miss Grandpa," Connor said and his voice hiccupped with emotion.

"I am too, buddy."

CHAPTER 12

elly rode in the passenger seat of her own minivan as they drove to his mother's house. There was a familiarity with it, and yet it felt strange.

She'd opted for her own car. What if Clara Stewart wasn't happy to see her on the day she'd lost her husband? What if Kelly were the person that set her off?

Ray reached for her hand, which she realized she'd had wrapped around her phone so tightly her fingers had gone white.

"Why are you nervous?" he asked.

"Who said I was nervous?"

"I say you're nervous. My mom is okay with you."

She nodded. It wasn't as if this was the first time she'd seen the woman in the past two years. "I just think that maybe you should have talked to her first. What if she just wants her family around her."

"You are her family."

"Was her family."

"Are," he said again. "For the record, my mother has never had an unkind thing to say about you."

"Really?"

"Really," he assured her as he removed his hand from hers just as her phone buzzed in her lap.

Kelly looked down at the screen. Jeremy's name flashed and she quickly turned it off, and made sure to silence it, just in case he called.

She wondered if Ray had seen Jeremy's name and her reaction. His fingers wrapped around the steering wheel tighter now, so she had to assume he'd noticed.

In the moments that they had shared together, created by Ray, he had slipped into a comfort, almost as if the past two years hadn't existed. In those moments, he forgot that she might be moving on. He just wasn't sure he wanted her to move on by going backward.

Ray had won her over in college, when Jeremy had broken her heart. But a year later, Ray had done the same thing, and Jeremy was there to pick up the pieces—only briefly. Kelly had come to her senses quickly, and she and Ray had mended their relationship, which then carried on for years before they were married and then had kids.

Would he be more comforted if she'd found someone new? He was afraid of what might happen if she got too involved with Jeremy Cross. Though he didn't expect her to petition to get her ex-husband back.

The rest of the ride to his mother's house was silent between them, as she fussed over the kids from time to time.

When he pulled the van in front of his mother's, he put it in park, and sat for a moment.

Kelly dished out instructions before the kids climbed from their car seats, and she gathered her purse, sliding her sunglasses to the top of her head.

Ray reached for her, taking hold of her hand, and stopping her progress. When she looked up at him, her eyes wide and compassionate, and he knew they'd have to talk about Jeremy—anyone but Jeremy.

"Thank you for coming with us," he said and her lips softened into a smile.

"I'm always here for you—all of you."

"That means a lot."

Connor unbuckled and moved up between the two front seats. "Is Grandma going to be sad and crying?"

"Maybe," Ray said. "Just hug her. She needs you both right now. You'll make her feel better."

They all climbed from the van. Kelly took her time to make sure the kids hadn't left anything in the van upside down, or messy, as the kids each held one of Ray's hands and walked toward the house. He heard the doors on the van close and he knew she was walking slowly up behind them as his brother opened the front door.

"She's been waiting for you," his brother Doug said as he stepped onto the porch to hold open the screen door.

Charlotte and Connor hesitantly crossed into the house as Ray hugged his brother before stepping inside.

"Hey, Kel," he heard his brother say and saw him pull her in for a hug when Ray turned to see her walk toward the door. "It's great to see you. You look great."

"Thank you," she said softly.

"Mom will be happy to see you."

Kelly walked into the house and Ray smiled back at her as he walked toward the kitchen where his mother sat at the kitchen table.

When she saw him and the kids walk through the door, his mother wiped her eyes and held her arms out for the kids.

Usually, they would have run into the house and right to her, but today held a different feel.

Connor moved toward her, holding his sister's hand.

"I'm so glad you're here," Ray's mother said as she scooped

them into her arms and kissed each of them on the head. "My cookie jar is filled for you."

That warranted a look toward their parents, and Ray noticed Kelly hold up two fingers, giving them permission.

As soon as the kids made the move toward the cookie jar, his mother smiled toward Kelly.

"Kelly, it's so nice to see you," she held her hand out to her for Kelly to take, which she did. "Ray said you sat with the kids last night."

Kelly kissed his mother's cheek. "I'm so sorry about George. And I was telling Ray, I'm here to help you with anything. I know there are so many plans, and I took the day off, and can take off more next week if needed."

Ray's mother placed her hands on Kelly's cheeks. "I appreciate all of that. Thank you. And I'm going to take you up on all of that. My heart is broken, and the less I have to think of, the better."

"Then I'm here for you," Kelly said as she shifted a gentle look toward Ray and his brother who had moved in next to him. "I'm here for all of you."

CHAPTER 13

*R*ay poured each of the kids a glass of milk, to go with their third and fourth cookies. Kelly sat at the dining room table with a notebook making phone calls for his mother. Doug had been in and out of the house. Much like Ray, he was doing his job from their mother's kitchen table.

His mother was cooking. She'd put on a soup made up of things in the refrigerator. Ray wasn't sure it would be an edible mix, but it was keeping her calm. Within a few hours, he was sure there would be relatives and friends dropping by.

Just as the thought crossed his mind, his phone rang and Alex's name crossed his screen at the same time Craig sent a text.

"I just heard about your dad. Catherine just called. Man, I'm so sorry," Alex said. It had been four years ago when Alex went through the same thing.

"Thanks. It was sudden."

"We're all here for you. Let me know what we can do."

Ray smiled. Since Coach Diaz had passed away in February, the guys he'd played college ball with had been a family again. He expected two more phone calls or texts just like the call he was sharing with Alex, and the text he'd received from Craig.

"I'll let you know. Kelly is here now helping Mom out with arrangements. Actually, Mom is cooking and Kelly is working."

Alex laughed. "My mom read a book. It kept her calm."

Ray stood from the table and let himself out the back door. "It's nice to have Kelly around. Mom's comfortable with her, and I miss having her near."

Alex let out a hum. "You sound a little smitten."

"Haven't I always been where Kelly is concerned?"

"And you got divorced why?"

Ray let out a breath. "Because some wise ass, who was tired, over worked, and broke, told a woman who was tired, over worked, and trying to help make ends meet that they should."

"You should kick that guy's ass."

"Oh, I have a feeling I'm paying for it. I think she's seeing Jeremy Cross again."

Alex took a moment. "That's the guy she dated before you and in between?"

Ray finally chuckled at that. "Yeah. His kids go to the same school as the kids. I knew she'd move on in time. I didn't think she'd move in that direction."

"You don't get a say in that, you know."

"I know," Ray agreed. "I also kissed her."

"When did all of this happen?" Alex asked.

"In the past six hours. Well, the dating Jeremy, I think that's been a few weeks. The kiss, that was this morning when she was sleeping in my bed."

"You need therapy. Can you get away tonight?"

"I'm sure I can. Doug is here. I'll have Kelly take the kids for the weekend."

"I'll get everyone together at our house."

"I'd appreciate that."

. . .

KELLY ROLLED HER HEAD FROM SIDE TO SIDE TO WORK OUT THE kinks that had formed from holding her phone to her ear for the past two hours. But in that time, she'd called the mortuary and made funeral arrangements. She and Doug had settled on a venue for the reception after the funeral. The minister had been notified, and would call on their mother that evening.

Looking over her notes, she had a few questions for Clara about the catering and the verse she wanted in the program for the funeral.

She was glad they'd let her help with the arrangements. It was a hard time to make decisions, and perhaps she was able to offer them some comfort by taking care of that.

When she looked up, Ray was leaned up against the doorway, his arms crossed, and he smiled at her.

"You look tired," she said. "You should lay down and get some rest."

"I just sent mom upstairs to do just that."

"Well, you didn't get any sleep either," she reminded him as she gathered her notes and closed her laptop. "I have some questions for her, but you can get the answers to me tomorrow. I'll get the kids together and take them home. I assume you'd like some time for your family."

"You don't have to hurry off."

"I'm not. I did what I came to do. All the arrangements are made," she offered as she slipped her laptop into her bag and gathered up her notes. "I'm glad I could do this much for her—for all of you," she amended.

Kelly walked toward him and stopped when she neared him. His eyes were red with dark circles under them. The day had taken its toll on him.

"Thanks for taking the kids. They've held up pretty well today, considering."

"They have a lot of questions."

"I'm sure they do."

"Everything is set for Wednesday," she said. "I'll come back by tomorrow and sit down with your mom and talk her through it all."

Ray reached for her and pulled her to him. He wrapped his arms around her, resting his head to her shoulder as she held him.

"You are, and have always been, the most caring person I have ever known," he complimented her.

Kelly closed her eyes and took in a breath. "I appreciate that. But he was a father to me for a long time. And your parents still always have treated me like part of the family."

Ray eased back and set his eyes on hers. "I said it earlier, and I'll say it again, you are family. You are the mother of their grandchildren, and a dear friend to them and me."

It still hurt when he said that, especially after being wrapped in his arms, and having tasted his kisses so many times throughout the day.

Ray dropped his arms and Kelly hiked the bag up on her shoulder as she started past him.

"Did you remember to call Jeremy back after he texted you this morning?" he asked and Kelly bit down hard before turning back to him.

"No. I'll call him some other time."

"I suppose he'll want to know why you weren't at work, huh?"

She pursed her lips. "He knows. He was there when you called."

His cheeks filled with color and his eyes had gone wide, but he reeled it in as he leaned against the wall again with his back. "I didn't realize I had interrupted your romantic evening."

Now the sweetness of Jeremy's touches and kisses seemed vile, and she moved closer to Ray. "I didn't say you did."

"You don't have to say it. As I'm reminded by my friends, it's none of my damn business who you see."

"That's right."

"But you've already been there and done that," he accentuated the word.

"Let it go, Ray."

"Sure. Sorry. We're not married. I don't get to worry about who you have around our kids."

It took everything she had inside of her not to smack him across the face.

"Do you need a ride home?" she finally bit out the question.

"I'll get a ride."

"Good," she said as she moved past him to gather the kids and head home. She was going to need to do some decompressing after the mixed bag of emotions Ray had opened up on her throughout the day.

CHAPTER 14

*C*harlotte was crying when they walked out of the house, and no doubt that was because of the mood Ray had put her mother into.

He knew in his heart he was the reason they were divorced, and here he was again pushing for a fight, when really there shouldn't be one.

"Kelly was a big help today," Doug said as Ray shut the front door to his mother's house.

"Sure."

"Something happen?"

Ray let out a snort. "Just my big mouth. It's not important." He ran his hand over his hair. "Funeral is Wednesday. I guess we just live in some form of limbo until then."

"Everyone in the world goes through this."

"Well, I wasn't ready to go through it," Ray snapped at his brother and then shook his head. "God, I'm so sorry."

"Don't be. Do you need a ride home?"

Ray nodded. "I'd really appreciate that. Can you be with her tonight?" he asked, looking up the stairs toward their mother's bedroom.

"I'll be here."

"Thanks."

IT DIDN'T SURPRISE RAY THAT WHEN HE PULLED UP TO ALEX AND Catherine's house, he could account for everyone's cars. His friends had gathered for him, just as they had done when Alex's father died, and when Rachel's father, Coach Diaz, had died earlier that year. But, then, he'd never have imagined they'd rally around him.

Catherine opened the front door to the house where she now lived with her husband Alex, who had bought the house from Rachel's husband Craig. Ray chuckled when he thought about the changes that had been happening since they'd all come together for Coach's funeral in February.

As he walked toward the house, Catherine stepped outside and embraced him the moment he was close to her.

"I'm so sorry about your dad," she said in his ear.

"I appreciate that."

"We can hold down the fort at work until you're ready to come back," she offered.

"I'll be there Monday. I can't stop living."

"But you need time," she reminded him.

"I'll let you know if I need anything," he said.

"Promise?"

"I promise."

Catherine settled on that with a nod before turning back to the house, opening the door, and waiting for Ray to step inside. When he did step into the house, everyone stood from their seats and moved to him.

There were hugs and a few brotherly slaps to the back. A lot of condolences and promises to help if he needed it. Ray knew each and every one of them was sincere.

Rachel walked out of the kitchen, now with a definite waddle as she progressed into her third trimester. She handed Ray the beer she carried in her hand, and pressed a kiss to his cheek.

"It hurts like a son-of-a-bitch, doesn't it?" she asked, and he knew she felt his pain.

"It does. Does it go away?"

"Nope. You learn to live with that dull ache."

Great, he thought. Just what his life needed, one more dull ache that was always there, like the one he lived with when he thought of the marriage he'd thrown away.

Everyone sat down in the small living room, and the air was filled with a silence that Ray was comforted with. No one knew what to say to him, but they were there together—they were all there for him.

Catherine rested her hand on his knee, drawing his attention to her. "Are plans in place?" she asked, and Ray lifted his eyes to her.

"Wednesday. I'll text you all the information."

"Did they have plans prepared?"

"Some, but Kelly stepped in and took care of everything for my mom." He let out a breath. "She was our savior."

Again, that awkward silence filled the room, as the group absorbed his sadness. Eventually, Alex turned on a college basketball game, and the mood eased.

As soon as the game was over, everyone began to disperse, but Ray didn't hurry out the door. He took his time to walk to the kitchen and throw his bottle into the recycle, and retrieve a bottle of water.

Opening the water, he watched Alex walk into the kitchen and repeat the steps he had just taken himself. When Alex opened his bottle of water, Ray leaned against the counter. "Thanks for having everyone over for me. This helped."

"That's what we're all here for, right? Brotherhood. I know it helped me when I came home for my dad's funeral, and you all were here for me."

"We should have kept up then."

"We were younger, and stupid."

Ray laughed at that. "A lot has changed since then," he said as he heard Alex's daughter on the baby monitor which was on the kitchen table.

Nodding his head, Alex let out a sigh. "You're right. A lot has changed. How are your kids doing with it?"

"There's a lot going on in their heads right now." Ray ran his hand over his head. "Connor, Dad, and I had plans for Sunday's football game."

"Ouch."

"Yeah. Then this morning when we were sleeping, in the same bed, the kids came in and woke us up."

"Was that when you were kissing her?" Alex asked, his brows raised, referring to the phone call they'd had earlier. "Before. I didn't kiss her in front of them. But, I suppose knowing your parents live in different houses, and see other people," he bit out, "and then they're in the same bed—it would confuse a kid."

"It's confusing me."

"Me too," Ray admitted as he lifted the bottle to his lips and sipped the water. "Lately, she's been on my mind a lot. Even before she stepped in to help me."

"But she's seeing someone else?"

Ray shrugged. "I don't know how serious that is."

"Maybe you should tell her how you're feeling before that other thing gets too serious."

Ray ran his hand over his stubbled chin. "And how stupid would I sound?"

"That's what you're worried about? You have feelings for a woman you married and have a family with, and you're worried about looking stupid? I think you looked stupid when you told her to divorce you."

And wasn't that the truth. "What if I'm just being emotional over my dad?"

"You said this was starting before this happened."

Ray finished the water in his bottle and then capped it. "We're not married for a reason."

"A valid reason?"

"What if it's just that I don't want her dating someone I don't like?"

Alex shrugged. "Is that what it really is?"

Ray blew out a breath. Now he wasn't sure. All he knew was he'd never stopped loving Kelly, even in the hard times.

Alex nudged him. "Why don't you go talk to her. Or just be around her. It would soothe you."

"Maybe I'll do just that."

CHAPTER 15

The afternoon seemed to have been more hectic than Kelly had expected. But, she was a big enough girl to admit, to herself, it was all in her mood.

Where did Ray get off telling her who she could and couldn't date? He'd stepped away from her. He'd decided their marriage wasn't worth it.

This wasn't something she wanted to hash out in her head. It had been two years, and they handled co-parenting just fine. So whatever was going on between them now was just Ray being out of sorts.

As Kelly loaded the dishwasher she could hear Connor and Charlotte arguing in the next room. "Would you two pipe down? I'm done listening to you argue."

For a moment the noise died down and Kelly could hear only the voices in her head again. Then the arguing resumed and she heard the lamp crash to the floor.

"What did you do?" were the first angry words that flew from her mouth as she stormed out of the kitchen and toward the living room where two wide-eyed children stood near the lamp on the floor.

"Charlotte bit me!" Connor yelled.

"He threw the pillow at me it and it hit the lamp. That's his fault," she argued back.

"Both of you…" The doorbell interrupted her thoughts.

Who in the hell was at her door at seven o'clock at night? Whoever it was, they weren't going to get a very warm reception, because now she was pissed. Not only was she replaying the past day in her head and the mixed bag of emotions between getting interrupted with Jeremy by Ray's call, to Ray kissing her in his bed, to him telling her who he approved for her, but now her own children were driving her crazy—and there was someone at the door.

"Don't move!" she scolded her children as she moved to the door and yanked it open.

On the other side stood two more children, wide-eyed, looking up at her as if she were some kind of madwoman, and Jeremy, his sexy warm smile lit on his face, had a hand on each of their shoulders.

"Did we interrupt?" he asked. "I knew you had a long day, and we thought maybe the kids could use some company. We brought *Moana*, popcorn, and some flavored water in lieu of juice or soda. What do you say?"

Kelly forced a smile to her lips and let out a breath. "I think that might be exactly what they need right now."

Kelly stepped back and Jeremy walked through the door, his hands still on each of his daughter's shoulders. The mortified looks on her own children's faces brought a pain to her chest.

"We had a little accident with the lamp," she said as she moved toward it to pick it up, handing the pillow to Connor to return to the couch. "The girls brought over a movie and some popcorn. Why don't you guys set up the pillows on the floor against the coffee table, like we usually do, and we'll watch the movie."

Connor and Charlotte moved slowly to do as she'd asked, as if they feared she might get mad at them again in front of the others.

Taking the bag of popcorn from Jeremy, she smiled up at him. "I'll go pop this and get some bowls. The DVD player is under the TV."

"I'll get the movie cued up."

As Kelly walked back to the kitchen, she rubbed her hand over the ache in her chest. Perhaps Jeremy had just saved her children from a lot of yelling that she had bottled up, and that wasn't their fault. Guilt washed over her. She sure was out of sorts.

She put the bag into the microwave and set it to pop. Then she pulled out the plastic bowls they used for movie night popcorn which were red and white striped. When the popcorn was finished, she carefully opened the bag and divided it between five bowls, figuring she could share with Jeremy.

Picking up four of the bowls, she carried them to the living room where the kids were set up, each with a bottle of flavored water, and a pillow at their back. Jeremy started the movie, and she handed each of them a bowl.

"Set your waters on the table behind you when you're not drinking them, okay?"

Four heads nodded in unison.

"I have to finish cleaning up dinner," she said. "I have one more bowl if you want to sit with them."

"I'll help you first," Jeremy said as he followed her to the kitchen.

"You don't have to."

"I want to."

Kelly walked back to the kitchen and to the dishwasher. She took the next plate from the sink and placed it in the washer. As she turned to pick up another, Jeremy was there handing it to her.

"Thank you," she said, putting it in the washer.

"You seem out of sorts," he offered as he handed her a glass.

"It's been a long day."

"Ray and his family—are they doing okay?"

"As well as you can when someone suddenly dies."

Jeremy touched her shoulder. "Kelly, I didn't realize . . ."

Kelly pursed her lips. "His father didn't make it through the night."

"I'm sorry to hear that. They're lucky to have each other. And they have you." He slid his hand from her shoulder to her arm turning her toward him. "He's very lucky."

The thought of kissing Ray and then the things he'd said when she left his mother's house mixed in her head as another man looked into her eyes.

"I owe it to the grandfather of my children to help."

"I'm just saying your character has always stayed the same. You're compassionate," he said pulling her to him. "You're caring." He brushed a strand of hair from her face. "You're the same lovely woman you were all those years ago." Dipping his head, he brushed his lips over hers until she eased against him, then he deepened the kiss and Kelly took what he had to offer. But her head swam with thoughts of their kisses that had been inter-rupted, the kisses Ray had fried her mind with, and back to what she was feeling in that very moment.

And though it was wonderful to have someone who thought so much of her kissing her and seeking that same reaction back, all she could think of was how Jeremy's kisses didn't even compare to Ray's.

CHAPTER 16

K elly could hear the laughter from the other room as Jeremy pulled her in tighter to her. What if her kids were to walk in? What would they think?

That morning they'd awoken to her wrapped in Ray's arms in his bed. Now, she was making out with Jeremy in the kitchen. What had she turned into?

As she eased back from him, she heard the knock on the door. A moment later she heard the squeal from Charlotte, "Daddy!"

The door opened, and Kelly distanced herself from Jeremy as if Ray had walked directly into the room.

Before she could make it out of the kitchen and to the front door, Ray walked in with Charlotte on his hip.

"It looks like I interrupted movie night," he said, with a forced smile on his lips.

"Moana," Charlotte said. "Come watch with me."

"I just need to talk to Mommy for a minute, but I'll kiss you goodbye."

Charlotte nodded as if the answer was sufficient enough as Ray set her back on the ground.

Jeremy moved toward Ray with his hand extended. "It's nice

to see you," he said. "I'm sorry to hear about your dad."

"I appreciate that. Kelly's been a big help getting all of the arrangements put together." His eyes were soft as they landed on her.

"I'm sure she has," Jeremy agreed as he placed a hand on her shoulder. "I'll let you two talk and I'll go sit with the kids."

Kelly tried to steady herself as Jeremy walked out of the room and Ray watched him.

"I didn't mean to break up whatever this is," Ray said, tucking his hands into the front pockets of his jeans.

"This was an impromptu drop by. He thought the kids would enjoy it after their hectic day."

"And it's very cozy in here," he offered as he stepped toward her. "Playing house?" he whispered.

"This is none of your business."

"Nope, it's not. I just needed another moment with my kids. It's still my week"

"And I'd never—ever take that away from you. You thought this would be better, remember?"

She watched him chew his bottom lip. "I remember. I'm sorry. I'm out of sorts. I'm in a mood."

"I thought you spent the evening with your boys. That didn't help?"

Ray rocked back on his heels and rested his shoulder against the wall. "It helped a lot. In fact, I suppose I'm only here to pick a fight."

"Aren't I a lucky gal?"

His eyes shifted toward the other room, and then back at her. "Okay, I really wanted to sit with you and talk. You bring a lot of comfort to me, Kel."

"I can ask them to leave."

Ray shook his head. "No. Don't do that. I'll kiss the kids goodbye and I'll see you on Wednesday."

"I need to stop by and see your mom."

"Why don't you come on Sunday? I think I'm going to take my brother and Connor to the game that Dad had the tickets for. I know Mom would still love to have Charlotte come spend some time, and Charlotte would be more comfortable with you there. You know, in the state things are in."

"Okay. Text me the information."

He stood there silently and she wondered what more he wanted to say.

"I'll do that," he said as he headed to the other room and she heard both of their kids hurry toward him and walk with him to the door.

By the time she'd made it to the door, he'd kissed them both, opened the door, and looked back at her with a gaze that said he needed her.

"Goodnight, Kel," he said as he stepped out of the door and closed it behind him.

Jeremy moved to her as the kids sat back down to watch the movie. "Everything okay?"

She forced a smile to her lips. "Everything is just fine."

"We could go in the other room and talk about it," he offered with his hand rubbing small circles on her back.

"I think I'd rather just watch the movie and then put the kids to bed. We've had a long day."

There was a flash of regret in his eyes. She was more than familiar with it, having turned him down many times in their past. But he nodded, and led her to the couch, where gratefully, Charlotte climbed up on her lap to cuddle.

RAY SAT IN THE DARK IN HIS LIVING ROOM. HE HADN'T TURNED ON the TV or the lights. He hadn't even poured himself a drink—not even water.

Solitude was what he needed in that moment.

He cried—sobbed.

He pounded his fists against the arms of the recliner.

He felt lost.

In the past twenty-four hours, he felt as if he'd lived multiple lives. When his mother called, he'd been the caretaker. When he stood and watched his father die, he'd been a little boy, now left alone in a big scary world. Holding Kelly in his arms, in his bed, had brought him immense comfort, and kissing her had nearly made him forget the pain that ripped through him.

At his mother's house, with his brother, he felt little again. How were they supposed to comfort her when they, too, needed comfort and reassurance?

His friends had given him that reassurance.

And what about his kids? They'd lost a great man. Did they understand the loss completely? Did they understand death and the impact of it? Did they understand he'd lost his daddy?

The tears came harder now, and he supposed he deserved the time to sit and cry.

But between the pain and anguish over his father, his mind would go back to Kelly and the comfort she could bring him. And then he'd think of her standing in the kitchen with Jeremy, his hands on her, and the air filled with something else.

She belonged to Ray, and there wasn't a man on earth that should be in his space.

The sobs turned to anger, and back to sobs.

He was lonely and in pain. These feelings for his ex-wife were just part of that. He could love her or hate her, but it wasn't fair to her to pull her in and push her away. And how much of it was real, and how much of it was grief?

Ray closed his eyes and drew in deep breath after deep breath until he was no longer crying.

He sat there for a while longer, until he felt completely numb. Then he dragged himself to bed, and with his clothes still on, he closed his swollen eyes and fell asleep.

CHAPTER 17

*K*elly argued with Connor over the number of shirts he was going to put on before he headed out into the cold to watch a football game.

"My T-shirt is fine," he said, pulling off the sweatshirt.

"Baby, it's November. It'll be warm one moment and snowing the next. You'll wear a long sleeved shirt, or the sweatshirt, which you can then take off and tie around your waist. You'll wear a hat and take gloves in the pocket of your coat."

"I have to wear my coat?"

"It's November," she repeated. "You can do what I say, or you can stay home. This is your choice, and I don't care that you're going with your father. You can miss it if you don't follow my rules."

"What if he says I don't have to?"

Kelly narrowed her eyes on him. "He'll say you have to, so you might as well do what I say."

Connor took the sweatshirt and tied it around his waist. Kelly gave him a nod, and walked out of the room to check on Charlotte who was dressed in her Elsa dress and had somewhere added lipstick to the look.

"Where did you get that?" Kelly asked as she watched her daughter crank the tube up all the way.

"In your bathroom."

"And are you supposed to go in my drawers?" Kelly asked as she took the tube from her daughter's hand before the tip wobbled off and into the carpet.

"I want to look good for Grandma. I'm going to sing for her when I get there, to cheer her up."

Her daughter sure knew how to defuse Kelly's anger. "I'm sure she will love that." She kissed the top of Charlotte's head. "Let's get going. Your dad is waiting for us."

"When are you going to get married?" Charlotte asked as she followed Kelly out of the bedroom, right on her heels.

"I'm not getting married," she said as Connor walked out of his room at that moment.

"Sammy said you are," he added to the conversation Kelly didn't want to have.

"Well, Sammy is incorrect. I don't plan to get married. I did that once."

Charlotte reached for her hand. "You can get married as many times as you want to. My friend Skyler's mom has been married three times."

Kelly winced at that. "I was married once. I don't want to do it again."

"Then why kiss Sammy and Sophie's dad?" Connor asked and Kelly turned to look at him.

"Why do what?" her voice cracked.

"I saw you kiss their dad the other night when we did movie night."

Kelly swallowed hard. The one thing she never wanted them to see was that. "It was a sad day."

"You didn't look sad."

Her stomach knotted. "I was. Can we not talk about this right now? We need to get in the van and get to your grandma's before your dad starts calling and wondering where we are."

RAY LEANED ON THE WROUGHT-IRON RAILING, THE NOVEMBER breeze numbing his skin. His brother had arrived with a brand new jersey for Connor, who was going to flip when he saw it. His mother had set up a high tea for Charlotte and Kelly at her dining table. She wasn't in the mood to go in public as they'd originally planned, but setting it up at home occupied her mind.

Neighbors and relatives had been dropping in on her, and his mother wasn't enjoying any of it. She wanted to be surrounded by family only. Doug was better at intercepting than Ray was.

Ray stood when he saw Kelly's van turn the corner. By the time he walked down the steps to the sidewalk, she'd pulled up in front of the house and parked.

He opened the side door as Kelly turned around toward Connor. "Don't forget that sweatshirt, and we're not going to discuss it again," her voice rose in pitch.

"What's going on?" Ray asked as he helped Charlotte out of her seat.

"Connor and I seem to be having an argument about appropriate wear for an outdoor football game in November."

Connor growled as he picked up the sweatshirt and crawled out of the van, stomping up the steps and through the front door of his grandmother's house.

Ray lifted Charlotte out of the van, set her on the ground, and shooed her up the stairs to find her grandmother.

"What's really going on?" Ray asked as Kelly gathered her things.

"They're just in a mood."

"They?"

She narrowed her gaze on him as she opened her door,

stepped out, and slammed the door purposely before walking around the front of the van.

"Are you accusing me of being in a mood?"

Ray shrugged as he closed the side door. "I'm saying it seems as if you're in a mood too, which I don't blame you. If they're worked up, it gets to us."

He watched as Kelly composed herself. "How is your mother doing?"

"You can ask her yourself."

"I'm asking you, so that I know how to handle her. Is she overly sad? Is she moving on day by day? Is she fine one moment and the next a wreck?" her voice still rose as she spoke.

"She's very excited to have Charlotte here, and you, too. She's grateful for everything you did to help get all the plans in order." He reached for her hand and held it between his. "I can't guarantee she won't cry, but it'll pass quickly. There's only moving forward, and she knows that."

Kelly pulled her hand back, and took a step to distance them. "Okay. I'll text you if Charlotte and I head home before you get back, and then you can drop Connor off at home. A football game is much longer than a tea party."

Yeah, he thought as Kelly passed by him and up the steps, Connor wasn't the only one in a mood. Perhaps there was some trouble in paradise, he snickered to himself, not wishing heartbreak on his ex-wife, but perhaps just enough that she didn't want to be with Jeremy Cross any longer.

hoever their dad had gotten the Bronco's tickets from, they were excellent seats. Three seats on the end of a row, fifty yard line, west side so the sun wasn't in their eyes as it descended, and a great crowd of fans surrounded them.

Connor had been just as excited about the jersey as Ray had thought he would be. And, they'd agreed he'd wear it over his coat, as the temperature had already begun to dip.

Uncle Doug had bought Connor a big orange finger, a soda, and a hot dog. Ray laughed each time they returned from a run to the bathroom and Connor had something new, but that was what single uncles were good for.

During half time, Connor switched seats with Ray to sit on the aisle, mostly because he wanted to flag down the guy with cotton candy.

"Have you checked on Mom," Doug asked as he finished off his beer.

"Didn't see a need to call. She's in good hands," Ray admitted. "Though, I guess that's if Kelly dropped her attitude."

"She had a 'tude?"

Ray shifted a glance at Connor. "They both did when they got there. Didn't you?" he directed the comment at his son.

"I don't want to wear the coat."

"But it's cold and going to get colder," Ray sided with his ex-wife. "Was the coat the reason you were fighting with your mom?"

"She was just in a bad mood."

"Why?" he pried a little more.

Connor shrugged his shoulders and put his feet up on the back of the chair in front of him. "Charlotte got into her lipstick and then asked her about marrying Sammy and Sophie's dad again."

Ray swallowed hard. "Why would Charlotte ask her that?"

He shrugged again and then tucked his feet under him. "Cuz Sammy said so, and then I saw them kissing."

Ray felt the blood drain from his head, and he found that the conversation made him stiffen too. "Mom is kissing him in front of you?"

Now he shook his head. "I just saw them. They were in the kitchen."

So he had walked into something when he'd dropped by, Ray realized, and the thought made him as sick as it had that night.

Again, he gave himself the pep talk about it not being his business, but it didn't work. He hated the idea.

When the cotton candy vendor walked toward Connor, Ray pulled out his wallet.

KELLY CARRIED CHARLOTTE INTO THE HOUSE, STILL IN HER ELSA dress. Tea with her grandmother had worn her out, or perhaps it was all the performing she'd done to entertain them.

Now she slept in her mother's arms as Kelly carried her up to her bedroom and laid her in her bed. She wouldn't let her sleep too long, or the entire night would be a bust. But Kelly needed a few moments to herself, so she'd let her rest.

She and Clara had had time to finish plans for the funeral and the reception that would follow. Then Clara gave her the Captain's uniform she wanted her husband to be buried in, and Kelly promised to take it to the mortuary along with photos of him.

Before she and Charlotte had left, Clara had pulled Kelly in and held her.

"My Ray made a mistake when he let you go," she'd said to Kelly. "In my heart, you're always going to be my daughter-in-law, no matter who else comes along."

Of course Kelly had cried the entire way home. Just one more reason to be grateful that Charlotte had fallen asleep.

Sitting down at the kitchen table, her laptop open and in front of her, she sent the few emails to finalize the funeral plans and to catch up on any work she missed..

When her phone rang, she answered it right away, as to not wake up Charlotte. When she said, "Hello," she realized she hadn't even looked at the caller ID.

"Kelly? This is Rachel Diaz, well it's Rachel Turner now."

"Rachel? It's nice to hear from you. I don't think I've seen you since college."

"We haven't. It's been a hot minute," Rachel laughed. "I do get to see your kids often, and I must say, I hope my kiddo is as well rounded and behaved as your kids."

Kelly felt the lightness in her heart. "Thank you. I appreciate that, and congratulations on your marriage and your baby."

"Thanks. Some of us take the long route to getting the guy," she laughed again. "I hope you don't mind that Ray gave me your phone number. I wanted to call and see if there was anything at all I could do to help with the funeral or the reception. Having gone through this not too long ago, I know how much work it is, and it's extremely nice of you to handle it for the family."

"I don't mind that he gave it to you at all. How nice of you to call," Kelly said looking at her chart of information for the funeral. "I'm not sure how much you can do. They had a funeral plan."

"God, that's smart. I'm going to talk Craig into that. I mean, hell, I have people shooting at me, so…" Rachel laughed, but Kelly sucked in a breath. The very thought of the story Ray had told Kelly squeezed at her heart, and it hit home too. Being in a school daily, she knew of all the precautions in place to keep the students and staff safe. She was well trained in active shooter situations.

"How are you?" Kelly asked. "I mean are you fully recovered?"

"Physically, yeah. The bullet went in and out of my shoulder, shattering it. Surgery rebuilt it, and I have new scars to cover with tattoos. Emotionally, I'm still working through it. But I'm a trained therapist. I know I'll be working through it for the rest of my life. And for my family, and myself, I will continue to do that."

"You're very brave."

"Nope, I'm human," she said on a sigh. "I'm in love and I'm building a family. It's amazing what you'll do to keep your family together."

Kelly heard the words and felt them pierce her heart. She covered her mouth with her hand to hold in the sob that nearly choked her. The reality was that she wasn't as brave as Rachel at all. She hadn't done everything she needed to do to keep her family together.

CHAPTER 19

*B*ecause she couldn't keep her emotions intact, Kelly let Charlotte sleep. It was dark, and all Kelly wanted to do was go to bed, but Ray was still out with Connor. She needed to take the time alone and pull herself together.

She hadn't quite had enough time to do so before she heard the soft tapping at the door.

Wiping her eyes, and tightening the ponytail she'd put her hair up in, she hurried to the door.

Ray stood with a grin on his face and a sleeping boy on his shoulder. A brand new Denver Broncos jersey covered the coat Kelly had fought with him to wear, and tucked between her son and his father was a bright orange, foam finger.

"He's worn out," Ray said as he stepped inside the house. "I don't know if he'll wake up or not."

"Charlotte is still asleep too," she admitted as she closed the door. "I'm going to have to wake them up for dinner and baths."

"I'll stay and help with that."

"You don't have to…"

"Kel, you have stepped in to help my family. You took off from work to help my mother, and you kept the kids so I could have some time. I certainly can help feed, clean, and put my kids to bed."

Kelly batted her weary eyes, soothing the sting of tears that wanted to break through. Ray passed by her to lay their son on the couch.

"Hey, kiddo. Wake up. Let's get this off you," Ray said softly as he knelt down in front of their son and helped him sit up. He pulled the jersey up and over his head, set it next to him, and unzipped his coat. As he eased Connor out of it, Connor's eyes closed again and he swayed away from his father.

"I don't think he's going to wake up," Kelly stifled her laugh.

"Why don't I just take him to bed. Hell, I'll come over early in the morning and help you get them ready."

"Ray, you don't have to do that."

He picked up Connor and winked at her as he started toward the steps.

Kelly wiped her eyes and fell into the chair next to her.

RAY HAD CHECKED ON CHARLOTTE TOO, AND SHE WAS FAST ASLEEP in her Elsa dress. The past few days had worn him down considerably, surely they had done the same for his children.

As he walked back down the stairs, he noticed Kelly sitting in the chair, her head rested back and her eyes closed. Yeah, it had been a busy weekend.

He should just let himself out and head home, but he wasn't ready to leave. Was it just the grief that made him want to spend time with Kelly, or was it jealousy? She wasn't his to be jealous over anymore, but he was.

Looking at this watch, it was only seven-thirty. Perhaps he'd stick around for a bit. After all, his name was still on the title to the house.

Ray walked through the kitchen to the refrigerator, where he knew Kelly kept cans of diet soda. He pulled one out, opened it, and looked at the pile she had on the kitchen table.

Her laptop was open and there was a stack of papers next to it. The teacher stamp set she'd use to put cute sayings on the papers for the kids in her class sat next to the papers. The notebook with her notes for the funeral was open too. Ray figured that was something he was privy to, so he picked it up and looked at it. She'd been finalizing plans, and the side of the paper was filled with the familiar doodles she'd draw while she was on the phone. Rachel's name was written on the paper too. She must have called Kelly, just as she said she was going to.

With his soda in his hand, he walked out to the living room and sat down on the couch. Kelly lifted her head, and with swollen, red eyes, she watched him.

"Sorry. I guess I'm tired too," she said as she rubbed her eyes.

"We're all exhausted. I saw your plan book in the kitchen. I hope you don't mind that I looked at it. Thank you for doing all of that for us. I know it has been a lot of help for my mom."

"It's what I could do. Have you eaten?" she asked and Ray laughed.

"Not as much as Connor did."

She smiled. "C'mon, I'll make us some sandwiches."

Kelly stood from her chair and walked back to the kitchen, and Ray followed. As she opened the refrigerator and pulled out items, Ray noticed the picture frame on the side of the refrigerator. He took it down and studied it.

"This is very sweet," he said looking down at the photo of himself and the kids at a school breakfast.

"The kids like to see you every day," she said as she set the items on the counter. "When you have them, I see them every day."

Ray hung the frame back on the refrigerator, only this time, he put it in the middle of the door. "Can we have a serious discussion?"

"Of course," she nodded as she continued to make sandwiches.

Ray leaned against the refrigerator and crossed his arms. "Connor told me that your bad mood this morning was because Charlotte said something about you getting married to Jeremy."

For a moment, Kelly stopped spreading mayonnaise on the bread. "I was just in a mood."

"Fine. Why does she think you're getting married? You're not getting married are you?"

Kelly set the knife down and turned to him. "If I were?"

That wasn't the answer he wanted, but fine. He'd go along with it. "Then I guess we'd all get used to the idea. But are you?"

She dropped her shoulders and turned back to the sandwiches. "No. I'm not getting married. His kids told our kids that, or so Charlotte said. I don't have any plans to get married again. I'm obviously not very good at it."

"So this thing between you and Jeremy isn't serious?"

She blew the strand of hair that fell over her eyes away. "I don't know what it is." She put down the knife again. "He's comfortable. I know him. He's arrogant, and then he's sweet. But when he kisses me," she paused and looked up at Ray, "I don't feel anything."

Ray's stomach tightened and his heart began to flutter in his chest. He thought about the conversation he'd had with Alex, and how he told Ray to tell Kelly how he felt about her.

Moving closer to her, Ray ran his hand over her shoulder and down her arm until he captured her hand in his. He saw her lip tremble before she bit it.

"I had a long talk with Alex the other day about all of this."

She lifted her eyes to meet his. "About what?"

"About you and Jeremy," he said and she looked away.

Ray cupped her face in his hands and drew her attention back to him.

"I thought I was being petty because I just don't like the guy," he snickered and she did the same. "Then I realized that wasn't it. And it's not because of my grief either."

"Ray, what are you talking about?"

He stepped in closer, until she had to put her hands on his chest to balance herself.

Ray searched her eyes for understanding, and in their softness, he was sure he'd found it.

"I've been thinking about you a lot."

"Ray…"

"Hear me out. Remember a few weeks ago I kissed you when you dropped off the kids. It was just so normal to me. It confuses things, but it was normal." Kelly nodded. "It's because you're always on my mind. The fact that we can be civil and friendly, well, that's always made me second guess my leaving."

"You think you made a mistake?"

He brushed his thumb over her cheek. "The moment the words came out of my mouth, I knew it was a mistake."

"Then why didn't we fight harder to save what we had?"

"Pride? Stubbornness? I don't know."

Tears welled in her eyes now. "You're sure you're not saying this out of grief?"

"I think my grief is making me see what I lost and what I need. And, Kelly, I need you."

"You need me to handle things. You need me around so you can see the kids all the time. You need me…"

"I love you."

The tears that had welled in her eyes rolled down her cheeks. "You love me?"

"I never stopped loving you. Never."

"You asked for a divorce."

"I was wrong."

She turned from him and opened the container of ham. "Ray, we can't do this."

"Why? Why can't we?"

Tossing the container back on the counter she turned to him. Now her cheeks were filled with color. This might have gone the wrong way, but it was in the open now.

"This is only going to confuse the kids more."

Ray shook his head. "Kelly, there is nothing wrong with admitting we made a mistake."

"I don't know if I can go through this again."

"You're not going to go through this again. If you give me a chance, I'll prove to you that I've changed." He stepped in again, brushing the loose strands of hair from her face and pressing a kiss to her cheek. "We can take it slow," he offered as he kissed her other cheek. "We can date," he said and she laughed.

"You want to date me?"

"I want to marry you again, but I know we need to take it slow." He kissed her forehead and her arms lifted around his neck. "Kelly, I love you." He kissed the tip of her nose. "Tell me when I kiss you, you feel something."

Her body softened against him and she let out a breath. "I feel something."

CHAPTER 20

*T*hose were the words he'd longed to hear. Ray wrapped his arms around Kelly's waist and pulled her to him before dipping his head to take possession of her mouth.

When she moaned, he knew she felt the same thing he did. This wasn't lust or sex. This was love, and they'd had that intimate sizzle between them since they'd met.

He'd been a fool to ever let her go.

Her arms tightened around his neck, and he eased her against the door of the refrigerator and deepened the kiss that already had his knees weak.

The kiss they'd shared the morning after his father had died had been nothing in comparison, he thought, as her mouth opened to his and his tongue sought out hers. This kiss had the heat they'd once shared, mixed with the emotions they fought to absorb.

He loved her. There had never been a day since he'd met her that he didn't love her. The past two years had been devastating to him, mostly because it had been him that had walked away and called it quits. He didn't deserve Kelly's compassion.

"Mommy," the small voice came from behind them and Ray

eased back slightly, pressing his forehead to hers as she caught her breath.

"Hey baby," she said softly and moved herself from underneath Ray, who took a moment to compose himself before turning around to look at his daughter in her rumpled Elsa dress. "Are you hungry? Daddy and I are having sandwiches."

Charlotte shifted her glance from Kelly to him and back again. He should have thought about what he was doing before he kissed Kelly. Sure, the kids could see them kiss and wake up in the same bed, but under the veil of divorce, that only confused things. And here he was worried Kelly was kissing other men in front of them. What was worse? Seeing their father in that situation with their mother and wondering why their family was still broken up, or seeing their mother move on?

Kelly held out her hand to Charlotte, who took it and walked with her mother to the table. She climbed up in her seat and Kelly finished the sandwich she'd been working on, cut it into four triangles, set it on a paper towel, and set it down in front of their daughter.

"I'll get you some milk to go with it. Would you like some grapes?"

Charlotte nodded to her mother and then again, shifted her watchful eyes to her father.

Ray pulled out the chair across from Charlotte and sat down. "How was your tea party with Grandma and Mommy?" he asked.

"Fine."

"Grandma made you special cookies. She showed them to me."

The furrowed brow of his daughter eased and she smiled. "They were dipped in pink icing and had sprinkles. I sang a song for Grandma and she didn't cry, even though she said she wanted to."

"Probably because she was so proud of you."

"Grandpa isn't going to come home now," Charlotte said as

Kelly set her grapes and a cup of milk on the table. "Grandma said he went to heaven."

Ray rested his arms on the table and clasped his hands as Kelly gave him a supportive smile and then returned to making more sandwiches.

"He did go to heaven the other night. The night when Mommy stayed at my house with you guys. I was with him when he went to heaven."

"Did you see him go to heaven?"

"Well, honey, just his spirit went to heaven where they say he'll get a new body that works, and he'll watch over us and keep us safe," he said, and then wondered if he were just adding to the expected lies people would tell their children.

"He'll watch out for Mommy too?"

Ray smiled. "Yes. He loved Mommy."

"Will he make it so that you and Mommy don't fight anymore and she won't marry Sammy and Sophie's dad?"

He saw Kelly lower her head as she finished their sandwiches.

"Would it bother you if Mommy married their dad?"

Charlotte shrugged. "I thought she was married to you, but you moved away."

"I only moved into another house. You know that. We're not married anymore."

"My friend's mommy has been married three times. She has three daddies."

Kelly turned to set their sandwiches on the table, then took the seat between Ray and Charlotte. "Daddy and I were married when you were born. But we decided we needed a break because things got very hard."

Charlotte took a bite of her sandwich. "Is it hard now?" she asked with her mouth full.

Ray shook his head. "It's a different hard, but we're older and wiser now."

Charlotte picked up her cup of milk with both hands, took a

sip, and set it back down before wiping the back of her hand over her lips. "I don't want Mommy to marry their daddy," she explained as she took Kelly's hand. "I don't like him."

He watched Kelly bat tears from her eyes. "Okay, baby. I won't marry him."

"Good. Why were you kissing Daddy?"

Ray eased back in his chair, letting his hand slide under the table and to Kelly's knee. When he did that, she turned to him, tucking her lips between her teeth.

Ray looked at his daughter, and now his son who had walked into the room and caught that last bit of the conversation.

"What if I told you I love your mommy very much? And what if I tried to be her friend, and maybe her boyfriend for a while?"

Charlotte nodded her head in full agreement, but Connor's sleepy eyes narrowed. "You kissed Mom?"

"I did," Ray admitted.

"She kissed Mr. Cross."

Ray lifted his brows. "Yes, she did."

"Aren't you supposed to be married if you kiss?"

He watched as humor lit in Kelly's eyes, but she kept her lips pressed together. "No, kiddo," Ray began, "you don't have to be married. People kiss to see if it's exciting and how they'd feel about each other."

Connor inched into the kitchen and Kelly pushed her sandwich toward him.

"How do you feel?" Connor asked.

This time Ray nudged Kelly's leg.

She shifted in her chair. "I care for your daddy very much. I would like to see if it might work out for us again."

Charlotte wiggled out of her seat and ran to jump into Ray's lap. He wrapped his arms tightly around her. But Connor kept his distance.

"So you can just always change your mind? I mean, you can

get married, and then you fight and one of you will go away again?"

And this was where even a six-year-old could make a man feel small.

Ray situated Charlotte on his lap. "Connor, I'm not going to move in. I'm going to be around more, and I'm going to see if your mom and I can work out our differences. I love her. I told her I love her, but you're right, I walked away and made a mess of things. I don't want to do that again. Will it be okay with you if we try that?"

"You'll be her boyfriend?"

"Yeah, something like that."

He walked to the table, picked up the sandwich Kelly had offered him, and took a bite. "Okay," Connor said as he swallowed. "But no more fighting."

"I can't promise that, but I promise that I'll work harder to understand why we're fighting and talk it out. Does that work?"

His son studied him thoughtfully as he took another bite. "Yeah."

CHAPTER 21

There was comfort in having Ray in the house, and hearing the noises coming from up the stairs as he bathed their children and got them ready for bed.

Kelly tidied up the kitchen, pre-packed lunches for the next day, and included one for Ray. She'd already decided he couldn't stay the night. They couldn't just jump right back into their life as if the past two years hadn't existed. In fact, she wished they hadn't gotten caught at all. Perhaps she needed some time to think it all over. Not that she didn't want Ray in her life. She hadn't said it, but she did love him. She'd never stopped loving him. But they'd messed everything up when they'd gotten divorced—everything. Was it wise to just think they could make it work?

When she heard the clomping of feet hurrying down the steps, she turned to see Connor and Charlotte, both with wet hair and clean pajamas, bound into the kitchen. A drenched Ray followed behind. Each of them wore a wide grin.

"We came to say goodnight, Mommy," Charlotte announced as she rushed to her and wrapped her arms tightly around Kelly's leg.

"Good night, sweetheart." She kissed the top of Charlotte's head before Connor nudged his sister out of the way.

He stepped up and wrapped his arms around Kelly's waist. "Good night, Mom."

She kissed the top of his head. "Good night, sweetheart. Sweet dreams."

As he pulled back he looked up at her as if he had something else to say, but instead, he only smiled and headed out of the kitchen.

Ray moved to her and kissed her gently on the lips. "I'll get them tucked in and situated. Then I'll head out."

Perhaps he understood their situation better than she thought. "That's probably for the best."

"I won't stay the night until your ready—until we're all ready."

Kelly considered that. It had been two years, she was more than ready. But logic played a big part in who she was. They still needed some time.

"I think that's wise."

He kissed her again, then disappeared up the stairs.

RAY WOULD NEVER TIRE OF TUCKING HIS CHILDREN IN AT NIGHT and kissing them before he turned out their lights. In the two years since he'd moved out, he made sure to call them each night when he wasn't with them. When they were at his house, he kept the habits he and Kelly had initiated before their divorce. Dinner, bath, and a bedtime story. He'd set aside enough time to talk to them before they went to sleep, and he'd check on them before he went to bed.

Kelly was straightening the living room when he'd cleared the steps, and when she lifted her head to look at him, he noted the worry that had flashed in her eyes before the smile settled on her lips.

He moved to her and pulled her to him. "I love tucking them

in," he admitted as he lowered his head to press a kiss to her exposed neck.

"Ray…"

"I'm leaving. I just wanted to do this for a few more moments."

Kelly dropped the pillow in her hand, and lifted her arms around Ray's neck as he moved his lips from her neck to her mouth and took it now without any hesitation.

Kelly eased against him and he was sure he could feel her heart beat.

As Kelly pulled back, she kept her eyes closed for a moment longer, before fluttering her lashes and looking up at him.

"Yep. I feel something."

Ray smiled down at her as he held her. "So do I," he dragged out the words. "We might need some time alone."

"I think that is wise. But, we have a lot to get through this week."

And just like that, he was brought back to the grief that he'd managed to push aside for a few hours. "It's going to be a long week."

"Your mom is doing better than I expected," she said as she rested her head to his shoulder. "But I suppose when the numbness wears off…"

"She'll be miserable."

"She's lucky to have you and Doug close by."

"And you and the kids," he reminded her as he shifted so she would look up at him. "This will make her happy."

Kelly smiled. "She told me that no matter who came along, I'd always be her daughter-in-law."

"I'd say we have her support then." He kissed her forehead. "I'd better go. Should we do dinner tomorrow?"

"I think they'd like that."

"Would you like that?"

She sighed. "I would. I'll make hamburgers."

"I'll be here." This time when he kissed her, he let it linger for only a few moments. "I'll see you tomorrow."

He took her hand and started for the door with her following him. Ray opened the door and turned back. "I'm sorry it took me so long to get to this point."

"Like you said, maybe your grief guided you to what was important."

He reached his hand to her cheek and held it there. "How could I ever have let you go?"

"We need time, Ray. We can't rush this."

"I know, but there is something in me that just feels free now that I told you how I feel. Who would have thought Alex would ever be the voice of reason?"

Ray stepped out the door and stood on the front porch looking in. At least this time when he left, he knew he'd be welcome back. He missed every part of his life in that house, even the bad parts. Now he knew they weren't so bad, and he'd just been weak.

He let out a breath, smiled, and walked toward his car. Kelly closed the door, and a moment later the living room light went off.

It would be hard not to rush back into what they'd had. All he could think of was walking back to the door, knocking, and sweeping her off her feet when she answered.

Patience. He'd had it before where she was concerned.

Ray started his car and backed out of the driveway. As he paused at the stop sign, he saw the lights of another car driving down the street. Easing through the intersection, he looked in his rearview mirror and it appeared as if the car had stopped in front of Kelly's house.

Slowing, he continued to strain his eyes as someone got out and walked to the house.

Once in the next block, he turned the car around and drove

back up the street. The front door was just closing, and he knew the damn car.

Ray slammed his hand against the steering wheel and let out a string of curses.

The minute he left the house, Jeremy Cross swooped right in, and she let him inside. What the hell kind of game was she playing?

CHAPTER 22

There was a chill in Kelly's classroom when she opened the door and turned on the light after having walked Connor to his classroom and Charlotte to hers.

She sipped from her travel coffee mug and set her bag on her desk.

"Good morning," her teaching partner Katie poked her head through the door and smiled.

"Good morning."

"Everything okay?" Katie stepped into the room. "I heard someone passed on Friday and that's why you were gone?"

Kelly leaned against her desk, her hands wrapped around the travel mug.

"My ex-father-in-law."

"I'm so sorry."

"He was a fantastic man," Kelly said pressing her hand to her chest when an ache formed there. "Ray had called me to be with the kids in the middle of the night on Thursday so he could go to the hospital."

"And his father didn't make it?"

Kelly shook her head. "I took Friday to help his family get everything in order."

"I don't know any divorced woman who would want to help her ex's family."

"It's not like that with Ray's family." She felt the smile widen on her lips. "They've always been good to me."

Katie watched her closely, and then pointed a finger in her direction. "What's going on with you? You should be sad."

"I am sad. I'm devastated."

"You're grinning."

Kelly sipped her coffee again and ran her fingers over the long necklace she wore. "Ray and I have done a lot of talking over the past three days, and we've decided to try and work things out."

Katie moved in closer to her. "You took back your ex-husband?"

"I'm going to. We know that we have to work our way into it. We can't just have him move back in as if nothing happened. The kids will need some time with this."

"I thought you were seeing the Cross kids' dad."

Kelly set her coffee on the desk. "I dated him in college and I've gone out with him a few times. It wasn't anything serious."

Katie nodded slowly as the bell sounded through the building. "I'm anxious to see how this all works out," she said as she turned to walk back to her own classroom.

Kelly picked up her coffee and took one more sip. Yeah, she was anxious to see how it would all work out too.

RAY HAD CALLED HIS MOTHER ON HIS WAY INTO WORK AND SHE'D cried the entire time. The thought had crossed his mind to not go into to work until Thursday. His mother needed him, and his mind certainly wasn't on work.

Now that he sat at his desk with an inspection report in front of him, he wished he'd heeded that thought.

He was missing his dad and wishing he could call him and tell him about the amazing time he and his brother had had with Connor at the Bronco game. Knowing how grief was pumping through his veins, he wondered just how much of that was to blame on his current infatuation with his ex-wife.

And wasn't that taking more thought than he cared for it to take?

Every time he thought of her, his chest ached. Oh, she was fully into them working things out until Jeremy Cross showed up to her door late at night and she'd let him in.

God, Ray thought, he'd been such a fool.

Maybe she'd just been telling Ray what he wanted to hear since she knew he was in mourning. Hadn't she even brought that up?

He looked at his watch, it wasn't even lunch time yet. There were hours left to stew over what had transpired the night before. Kelly was going to have a lot of explaining to do.

Ray was pulled from his destructive thoughts when he heard the knocking on his open door.

"Hey, pal," Alex stood in the doorway with his daughter on his hip. "We came to take Catherine to lunch. Can you join us?"

Ray ran his hands over his hair. "I don't think I'd be very good company today. But you guys take her and take your time. She's been working extra hard."

Alex stepped into the office and closed the door. "Everything okay? You look frazzled."

"I am," he could admit to his friend. "Mom was a mess today. She's held it together all weekend, but today…"

Alex sat down in the chair in front of Ray's desk and adjusted his daughter on his lap. "I think there is a numbness that carries you through for a few days. I remember having it when my dad died."

"I just want to get to Wednesday and get that part over. Then maybe the healing can start."

"We'll all be there for you," Alex promised. "And what about you and Kelly?"

Ray sat back in his chair. "I took your advice. I'm not sure it did any good, but the dialogue was opened."

"Like I said, we'll all be there for you, and I don't mean just at the funeral. Lean on us when you need to," Alex offered as he stood with his daughter. "Are you sure you won't join us for lunch?"

"I'm sure. Thanks for the invite and the visit."

"Guys' night at Toby's on Thursday?" Alex asked as he opened the office door.

"I'll need it for sure."

"Call if you need anything." Alex took his daughter's hand and had her wave goodbye, and Ray smiled at the gesture.

He leaned back further in his chair as Alex disappeared and thought about the week ahead. There was no way he could focus on the work that covered his desk. As soon as Catherine returned from lunch, Ray was going to head out, and he wasn't going to return until after the funeral.

He needed time to sort out his jumbled mind. He'd head over to his mother's house first and make sure she was taken care of before he spent the evening with his family.

There was no guarantee on how that was going to turn out. Every time he thought about Kelly and the plans they'd made, he grew angrier. But he'd told Connor he'd try not to make things difficult and not fight with his mother. He just wasn't sure he could make that happen, not after last night.

$\mathcal{U}$sually Kelly would change out of her school clothes into comfortable yoga pants and an oversized, long sleeve T-shirt. Her hair would be pulled up, and when the kids took their baths, she would wash off her makeup.

Tonight, however, she was still dressed, had touched up her makeup, and was whistling while she formed hamburgers. Connor had asked to help, and she'd gladly let him shape his hamburger into any shape he wanted.

"You look nice, Mom," he said as he reshaped his burger from a heart into a star.

"Thank you."

"Are you trying to look nice for Dad?"

Kelly chuckled at that. "I suppose that crossed my mind."

Connor reshaped the burger into a perfect circle and set it on the plate. "I'm okay if you get back together. It would make me happy."

Kelly pressed a kiss to the top of her son's head. "It would make me happy too," she said just as the doorbell rang.

"I'll get it," Connor hopped off the step stool.

"Whoa, your hands are covered in meat. You have to wash them."

"He's at the door."

"He'll understand," she argued as she turned on the water and added soap to both of their hands.

Connor washed off his hands, grabbed the towel on the counter, and ran for the door. Kelly laughed as she washed off her hands and waited for the towel to come back.

As she stood over the sink letting her hands drip, she heard the door open, and Connor squealed when his father scooped him up. Her heart raced a little faster, and she felt the smile widen on her lips.

She felt it—and it wasn't even in the form of a kiss.

RAY SET HIS SON ON THE GROUND AND FOLLOWED HIM TO THE kitchen. Before they entered, he drew in a deep breath. He couldn't be upset around the kids, he reminded himself. But before he left for the night, he was going to have his answers.

Connor ran back through the kitchen with the towel and handed it to his mother.

"Thank you," she said on a laugh and her eyes sparkled as she looked toward Ray.

He hadn't expected that.

She was still dressed as if she'd only just gotten home from work. Her makeup was on, though she'd pulled back her hair. In that very moment, he realized he appreciated her beauty, no matter if she was dressed up and made up or if she was clean faced and comfortable.

"Hey," seemed to be the only thing he could say without it sounding angry.

"Hey," she returned and the sparkle that had lit in her eyes, resonated in her smile. "Connor and I just got the burgers formed. The grill is hot. Charlotte asked to mix the juice for dinner."

"I'll cook up the burgers," Ray offered, figuring it would give him a few moments alone on the back porch to collect himself.

Kelly handed him the plate of burgers and the spatula. As he took it, she rested her hand on his arm. She knew something was eating at him, but did she know? Did she know that her actions from the night before had cost him a night's sleep and a day's work?

Ray took the plate and walked out the back door to where the grill steamed against the chilled November air. He lifted the lid, set the burgers on the grate, and looked around the yard.

He'd spent hours in that yard mowing, planting, and building the play structure that still stood in the shadows. Ray had been the one to walk away from it all when it had gotten too hard. What had he been thinking? How was it he was such a weak man that when time was scarce and money was tight, he had turned that into a problem between them. Why hadn't they taken the time to work through it? He still should have been mowing that lawn, and his wife shouldn't be seeing other men.

When the door opened, he turned to see Kelly standing there. She closed the door behind her, wrapped her arms around herself for warmth, and leaned up against it.

"Are you doing okay today? You look preoccupied," she observed.

"I'm fine."

"How is your mom?"

The breath he let out carried on the cold air. "Today was hard. She's been a bit of a wreck."

"I'd thought about calling her. Maybe I should have."

"I left work early and went over to be with her. I'll spend the day with her tomorrow too. Catherine said they can handle everything at the office until I can get back in after the funeral. I wasn't too productive this morning anyway."

She moved to him, and as if it were the normal thing to do, she wrapped her arms around his waist and rested her head against his chest.

"I can't imagine how hard this is on you," she said. "I wish I could be of more help."

Hesitantly, he wrapped his free arm around her. "You've done more than anyone expected. You're making it easy on us."

"It's what I can do." She eased back and looked up at him. "But is that all that's bothering you?"

The cold air now burned his lungs and he realized he'd been breathing it in too deeply, trying to remain calm.

"When we put them to bed, we can talk about it."

He'd heard the tone he'd relayed that with, and she must have sensed its anger. Kelly eased back and stepped away from him.

"Okay. I'll go help them finish setting the table. Charlotte drew us placemats. She thought it was a special occasion."

"That was sweet."

"They're very happy to have you here."

Ray chewed his bottom lip. "I miss them, Kel. I know I get to see them a lot, but I miss them."

She nodded in the glow that came from within the house. "Whatever is bothering you, don't let the kids see it. You can tell me all about it later."

Kelly disappeared back into the house and Ray closed his eyes and fought for that control he was going to need.

He knew he had to handle the situation just right, or he'd lose her again forever. But he didn't want to be lied to.

CHAPTER 24

*R*ay cleaned up the kitchen as Kelly got the kids bathed. They'd promised them a Disney movie before bed, and because it was still new enough, they both wanted to sit on the couch, between their parents.

As Lightning McQueen raced around the track, Ray looked at his family. Charlotte had only been two when he'd walked out the door, and Connor had been four. In their short lives, they hadn't had their parents together, well, not when they would have remembered it.

Money would be tight again. Owning a business never guaranteed success and steady income. Teachers were never paid what they were worth, even with a masters degree.

They were going to have misunderstandings.

They were going to fight.

They were going to have to get to the bottom of her letting Jeremy Cross into the house after he'd left last night, or he was going to explode.

Ray untucked himself from the couch and walked to the kitchen. Pulling the bottle of Tylenol out of the cupboard, he opened it, and poured two in his hand.

He took down a glass and filled it from the sink. Popping the pills into his mouth, he swallowed them down with the water. Still standing over the sink, he set his glass in it, and then stood, with his hands rested on the counter.

"You're going to have to tell me what's bothering you before you explode," Kelly's voice came from behind him.

"Not while they're awake," he said.

"So this isn't about your dad. This is about us."

He'd discredited her once, but she was always more intuitive than he cared for. She knew what went on in his head, so he was surprised she didn't just bring the subject up herself.

"When they're in bed, we'll talk."

He'd never turned around, but Ray heard her walk away.

When the movie was over, there were requests for another. Those requests were denied, and Kelly walked the kids up the stairs. Ray took a few moments to himself before joining them.

The process took nearly a half-hour to get them settled, answer all their questions, and make sure all the right stuffed animals were in position.

When Ray pulled Connor's door closed, he let out an exhausted breath.

He could hear Kelly in the kitchen, and he knew his mood had rubbed off on her. The kids would surely be awake in no time if she kept making that much noise.

Ray walked down the stairs and turned into the kitchen, just as Kelly pulled a paper towel from the roll and wiped her eyes. Yes, his mood certainly had worn off on her.

"Are you okay?" he asked from a distance.

"Fine."

And there he had his answer. No woman was ever fine, just because she said she was.

"If you're fine, why are you crying?"

She turned to face him. The makeup that had enhanced her eyes, now darkened them with smudges.

"All of that stuff you said this weekend was just crap, wasn't it? I mean, you said that your grief was making you realize what you'd lost, but that was all a lie."

Ray set his jaw. "I never lied to you."

"Are you just like your mom, and four days later you're finally feeling the loss? Was I helpful, Ray? Was I just in the way? Or was I just the distraction you needed?"

"I thought it was what I wanted. That didn't come from just losing my dad," his voice had begun to rise. "I've been thinking of you—of us, for a long time," he made sure he spoke in a hushed tone now.

"Really? Because today you seem as if you've second guessed everything you've said for the past few days. And you already told the kids, so you'll be breaking their hearts. They don't know us together, they only know us apart."

"And that's all my fault?"

"You wanted the divorce."

"You didn't try to stop it."

And with that they both stood and stared at each other, perhaps waiting for the other to accuse again.

Kelly wiped the paper towel over her eyes again as they welled with tears. "You're right. I should have fought harder for a marriage I was fully committed to. I never wanted you to go, but I couldn't argue with you anymore either."

"And I had to go."

"Now where are we?" She held up her hands and waved that comment away. "Never mind. I know right where we are. This was the wrong time for us to try and work this out. You need to focus on your mom and your brother. It's selfish of me to think we were right to try and fix years of—of whatever happened."

Ray ran his hands over his stubbled cheeks. "This is amusing. You think my mood over this is all because of my dad?"

"It's not? Ray, that's a huge loss. I don't blame you for saying things and then rethinking them."

"What about you? You say things and then go behind my back and stab me?"

Her eyes went wide with that. "I what?"

Ray moved toward her, and it ached in his chest when she took a step back. "You're promising me that we'll work on this. You know I love you, and yet you're just stringing me along."

"How can you say that?"

"Because I saw him come over last night after I left and you let him in and closed the door," his voice had risen loud enough it echoed in the kitchen.

Kelly sucked in an unsteady breath. "You were spying on me?"

"Oh, hell, the door hadn't even closed behind me before you let him in. So, you're going to take me back to appease the kids, and you're going to keep him on the side to appease you?"

With that, her hand whizzed through the air and across his face. "You are one selfish son-of-a-bitch, Raymond Stewart!" She screamed and sobbed at the same time as he put his hand on his cheek to ease the sting. "I didn't invite him in to take him to bed, hide him from you, or keep him to myself. He just showed up. I thought it would be the decent thing to tell him that I was going to work on putting my marriage back together and that I wouldn't be seeing him again."

Ray felt the blood drain from his face. "Kel…"

"What kind of whore do you think I am, Ray? I haven't slept with anyone since the last time I slept with you. And you think I'm just going to keep someone in my home when my children are here?"

She turned from him and rested her hands on the counter.

"If you don't trust me, just get out," she growled. "They'll understand, and things can just go back to normal. I'll have them at the funeral and the reception, and I'll have them back to you on Monday. I won't even come into the office. I wouldn't want to interrupt your very important time with them."

"Kel…"

"Just go home, Ray. I can't be with someone who second guesses me."

CHAPTER 25

*R*ay watched as Kelly fled from the kitchen and up the stairs. She slammed her bedroom door, and he wondered if she'd meant to or if she just couldn't help herself. But a moment later, he heard the other two doors open and he pressed his fingers to his eyes.

He turned off the light in the kitchen and walked toward the stairs where Connor and Charlotte both sat.

"You said you weren't going to fight," Connor reminded him.

"I said I couldn't promise. But I said I'd work on it if we did. But for tonight, I think I need to leave her alone. I've made her mad enough that I don't think she'll talk to me right now."

Connor's brows drew together. "Why did you do that?"

Ray shook his head. "Because I accused and didn't ask questions. I'm not perfect, kiddo. I have a lot to learn, and I'm not getting any younger."

Charlotte squeezed the stuffed unicorn in her arms. "Does this mean Mommy doesn't like you anymore?"

"I think it means I hurt Mommy's feelings and I'm going to have to apologize. But for now, let's get you both back to bed. I should go home."

"Why can't you stay here?" Charlotte asked innocently.

"It's not time. I have a lot of emotional things happening all at one time. I need to learn to separate them so I can do right by everyone."

Ray started up the steps and Connor rose, and crossed his arms. "Are you picking fights because Grandpa died?"

Ray smiled and shrugged his shoulders. "I might be. I'm very sad right now."

"I'm sad too."

"I know you are. So is Mommy. She loved Grandpa and he loved her too, like a daddy loves a daughter." He reached for Charlotte's hand and helped her to her feet. "I need to let your mommy know that I love her always, and not just because I'm sad right now."

Connor continued to study him. "Maybe you need a time out to think about what you did."

The thought made Ray chuckle. "Sweetheart, that's exactly what I need. Now, let's get you two to bed so I can go home."

KELLY PRESSED HER FOREHEAD TO THE BACK OF HER BEDROOM door and let the tears roll off her cheeks. She should open the door and take him into her arms, but she couldn't.

Ray needed to sit with the thoughts he'd had, but she'd heard his regret when he told the kids he loved her.

They could make this work, she thought as she walked to her bed and crawled under the sheets. In time they could be a family again, but he was right, he was lashing out because he was sad.

Kelly wiped away the tears and listened for the front door to close. When it had, she closed her eyes and tried to sleep. But sleep would elude her with thoughts of possibilities and failures as they tried to move forward as a family.

∾

KELLY HAD SPENT HER LUNCH BREAK ON TUESDAY, AND AFTER school, following up on items for the funeral. She wanted to make sure everything was in place for the family, no matter how angry she was with Ray.

As she looked at herself in the mirror on Wednesday morning, dressed in her black dress and pearls, she realized just how tired she looked.

Sleep hadn't come to her since she'd asked Ray to leave. He'd texted his apologies and left her a few voicemails, but at the moment, she just didn't want to talk to him.

Connor stood in her doorway, dressed in the new suit Kelly had bought him just for the funeral. "You look very handsome."

"Will Grandma be happy to see me in this?"

"I guarantee it," she said as she held out a hand to him to join her. "You look just like your daddy in that suit."

"Is that good?"

Kelly kissed his cheek, and then wiped away the lipstick that she'd left. "It's very good. Your daddy is very handsome."

Connor looked down at his shoes. "You were fighting with him again."

It had taken two days for him to say something about it directly to her, even though she'd heard him talk to Ray about it that night.

"I was. It'll all be okay. Daddy and I have a lot of things to work out."

"I want him to move back in here with us," Connor said. "Charlotte doesn't remember him living with us."

The very thought squeezed at Kelly's heart. "I'm not ready yet. We need to work up to that."

"Will you get there?"

"That would be the hope, right?"

"Daddy's sorry for whatever he said," Connor assured her.

"I know he is," she said as she pushed away hair from his forehead. "Let's go see how Charlotte is doing and head out. Grandma will need a lot of extra love today."

"And Daddy and Uncle Doug too?"

"Yes, and Daddy and Uncle Doug too."

Connor took her hand and they walked to Charlotte's room. She had tied a bow around her unicorn's neck and asked to take him too. Kelly agreed. Everyone needed something to get them through the day.

As the three of them walked down the steps, the doorbell rang. When Kelly pulled open the door, her mother and father stood there, both dressed in black.

She fell into their waiting arms. "What are you doing here?" she sobbed at the sight of them.

"We came to pay our respects," her mother said as she patted Kelly's back. "He was your family."

"You should have told me you were flying in. I would have picked you up from the airport. You could have stayed here."

"Honey, I know you're helping Ray's family through all of this. We're grownups. We can take care of ourselves. And you look beautiful," her mother said before she scooped up Charlotte, and pressed a noisy kiss to Connor's cheek.

Kelly wiped away her tears. "I'm just so happy to see you."

Her mother set Charlotte back down and took Kelly's hands. "We're here for the week. And this weekend we'd love these two to spend it with us."

Both Connor and Charlotte looked up at her with wide eyes. "Please," Charlotte pleaded.

"We'll be really good," Connor promised.

Kelly let out a grateful laugh. "Of course."

CHAPTER 26

*W*ith her parents offering to help, Kelly let the kids ride with them, and she left for the church so that she could be there to make sure everything was in order.

The hearse was parked in front of the church. A quick look at her watch told her that the family cars would be arriving shortly. Clara had asked that the family have time to say goodbye before others arrived.

As Kelly stepped out of the car, the family car pulled into the lot. She stood and watched as Doug stepped out of the car, helped his mother, and Ray followed. In the next car that arrived was George's brother and his wife.

Ray smiled at her as his family walked toward the church, and he walked toward Kelly.

"You look beautiful," he said as he neared her.

"And you look handsome."

"Where are the kids?" he asked looking toward the car.

"My parents are here. They'll bring them."

"I didn't know they were going to be in town."

Kelly shrugged. "They showed up this morning. They flew in for the funeral."

Ray blew out a breath and a tear rolled down his cheek. "That was very sweet of them."

"You'd better go inside. I'll make sure everything else is in order."

Ray reached for her hand. "I'm sorry, Kel. I was out of line the other night."

"Today isn't the day to think about that."

"I think it's the perfect day for it. Today reminds us that tomorrow is never promised," he said as he sniffed back tears. "I was an asshole the other night. In fact, I've been an asshole for a long time. I'm tired of being that guy."

"You can reflect on that after the funeral. You need to get inside."

With her hand still in his, he interlaced their fingers. "And you're coming with me. You were his daughter for a long time. Mom wants you with the family, and Dad wouldn't have it any other way."

She studied his sad eyes. She still wanted to be mad at him, but today needed to be all about him and his family.

Hand in hand, they walked toward the church to say goodbye to a great man.

WITH HIS MOTHER BETWEEN HIM AND HIS BROTHER, RAY HADN'T let go of Kelly's hand since he'd taken it in the parking lot. For some reason, it felt as if too much rode on her being there. If he let her out of his sight, he thought he just might lose her. Then again, he was sure it was the emotions of the day just kicking him in the ass.

His father lay in the open casket and his mother wept.

The comfort of Kelly's thumb brushing over his knuckles kept him calm.

People filed into the church and filled pews, men dressed in uniform, whom Ray recognized from the days when his father was a fire fighter. Then, Ray turned, as if he'd felt them, and watched as Alex and Catherine, Rachel and Craig, Bruce, and Toby all took their seats with Alex's sister Sarah right behind them.

He let out a sigh and nudged Kelly to look back. She gave them all a wave and turned her attention toward her parents and their children taking seats behind them.

When his mother noticed them, she turned, and both kids moved in behind her to kiss her cheeks, and then Kelly's mother did the same.

His whole world was right there in that room. His friends. His parents. His brother. His children. His wife.

The last thought struck him in the chest. Once again, he'd nearly pushed her away because he hadn't taken the time to stop and think.

Sobs coming from his mother pulled him from his thoughts.

If he didn't stop being so selfish when things got hard, no one would be sobbing at his funeral. His father was unconditionally loved by his mother, who weathered many storms with him.

They fought a few times a year, those kinds of fights that ended with broken glasses and nasty words. But at the end of the night, they'd slept in the same house, if not the same room. Why did they fight, for the same reasons he and Kelly had fought years ago? Kids were hard to raise, and they hadn't even gotten to the hard stuff yet. Times were tough and money was hard, just as it had been for him and Kelly.

Now his sobs began and Kelly's hand came apart from his and wrapped around his shoulders as she pulled him to her.

Of all the times he'd listened to his parents fight and then make up, he'd forgotten that there was a light at the end of the tunnel. Instead, he'd walked away.

How could she ever forgive him for that or assume he'd never do it again. Even once they'd decided to mend things, he threw out accusations. When would he learn? Would she be there to sob at his funeral?

Ray closed his eyes and tried to catch his breath. When he opened them again, Charlotte walked toward them, having left her grandmother to sit on her father's lap.

He was surrounded by love at that moment and he mourned more than just the loss of his father. He mourned his sensibility and the life he shouldn't have walked away from.

With Charlotte wrapped around him, her little arms around his neck and her cheek pressed to his chest, he reached for Kelly again. This was a huge loss for him, his father's death, but he was going to use it as a wakeup call.

As the minister stood before them and began his sermon, Ray gave Kelly's hand a squeeze. When she looked up at him, her eyes damp with tears, he smiled at her and mouthed the words, *I love you.*

CHAPTER 27

*T*he sermon concluded. The casket was closed.

Kelly felt the air shift as the family stood from the pew to be led out of the church and to the waiting cars. As Ray stood, she continued to sit.

He turned to her and reached out his hand. "C'mon."

"Ray, you should go without me. I'll follow."

He shook his head. "I want you with us. They want you with us. Please."

She looked back at her mother who gave her a nod while holding Charlotte on her lap.

It was a stupid time to wonder what people would think of seeing them together, holding hands. Everyone knew they were divorced. Would they think she was some gold digger? Not that there was gold to be dug. Was she seeking attention?

She took Ray's hand and walked out with them, in front of a church full of people. The family filed into the car and when they were closed inside, Ray's mother let out a breath. "I didn't think this day would come so soon. I mean, I thought I'd be much older," she admitted.

No one said anything, but Doug put his arm around his mother's shoulders.

When Clara had composed herself, she wiped away her tears. "Kelly, thank you for all your help. I'm sure we could have managed it, but it was a blessing to have you here."

"I'm glad I could help," she said as the car pulled away, following the hearse, and leading the procession to the cemetery.

WHEN THE FUNERAL HAD CONCLUDED GRAVESIDE, KELLY STOOD TO the side with Connor and Charlotte, each one holding her hand, while Ray, his mother, and brother greeted everyone.

When the line moved and his friends were next to reach him, Ray opened his arms and the other four men huddled around him.

Alex slapped him on the shoulder. "You doing okay?"

"We're going to be fine. I'm still shaken up."

Rachel stepped up to him and hugged him as much as she could, her enlarged belly keeping him from picking her up to hug her. "I don't know if you believe in heaven or not, but I think your dad and my dad will be fast friends," she said and it brought comfort to him.

"I think you're right."

"It's nice that Kelly's here and was with the family," Rachel lifted her brows.

"If I don't screw everything up, we're going to try and work it out."

Rachel smiled wide. "That's very exciting. I'm going to go talk to her."

Ray hugged each of his friends again and then watched as they extended their condolences to his brother and mother, and then walked toward Kelly.

He watched as each of them hugged her and shook Connor's hand. Charlotte hid her face against Kelly's leg. As they dispersed,

Rachel and Catherine continued to talk to her. He wondered what could be transpiring when Kelly smiled and nodded.

AFTER THE SERVICE AT THE CEMETERY, THEY WENT BACK TO THE hall adjacent to the mortuary and Kelly guided guests through the reception as Ray and his family, again, spoke to all of the people who had joined them to mourn his father.

As the crowd dispersed, and Kelly's parents drove away with the kids, he moved to her.

"I just realized the family car picked us up at Mom's, but your car is at the church."

Kelly nodded. "I should have left with my parents."

"You were too busy making sure everything went just right. Thank you for that. And I'll give you a ride," Ray offered, desperately wanting to pull her close to him, but he refrained.

"Thank you. It was nice all of your friends came. A little overwhelming, but nice."

Ray chuckled. "I suppose that could be overwhelming. Rachel was excited to talk to you."

Kelly smiled. "She and Catherine invited me out for margaritas and nachos tomorrow night. She said it's guys' night at Toby's and girls' night out."

"It is," he confirmed. "I take the kids with me when I have them. Toby's house is really just a big fun house."

Kelly laughed and Ray found that it lightened the heaviness in his chest. "I've heard."

"I can take both of them with me. No one gets out of control or anything."

"I haven't decided if I should go with them yet."

"Why? You'll have a great time."

"Why? I know we said we'd work on this, but I feel as if I'd be under a microscope. I don't know Catherine really at all, and Rachel was only an acquaintance. I don't fit into your circle, Ray."

"I think the invite was their way of saying you do," he offered and then took her hands. "Go. They're very important people to me, and so are you. Besides, Rachel could use more friends, and so could Catherine. Perhaps two of the least maternal people are mothers, and they could use someone to guide them. I can't think of anyone better than you for that job."

Kelly shook her head, but smiled. "Fine. I'll go. And, if I can convince Charlotte to go with me, I'll take her."

"She'd enjoy a grown up girls' night."

"I think she would, especially if Catherine brings the baby."

THE FAMILY CAR DROVE THEM TO RAY'S MOTHER'S HOUSE, AND AS promised, Ray drove Kelly to her car at the church.

"Do you think your parents will hold on to the kids for a few more hours? I'm just not ready to go home yet," Ray admitted as they sat in his car in front of the church.

"Of course they would. What do you have in mind?"

"An early dinner. I never did get to have any of the food served."

"You had a lot of conversations with people," Kelly mused.

"Doesn't it suck that a death is what brings everyone together?"

"It makes a statement, I suppose."

Ray nodded, running his hands over the steering wheel. "Will you have dinner with me?"

"Yes."

"And now that we're alone, and the day is over, can I apologize again for being an ass?"

Kelly smiled sweetly at him. "Apology accepted." She rested her hands in her lap. "Mom and Dad asked to keep the kids this weekend," she said looking down.

"I'll bet they miss them."

"They do. But I was thinking," she swallowed hard, "that

maybe I could make dinner on Friday night and you could come over."

Suddenly he didn't feel as cold in the November chill as he had. "I would like that."

"It'll give us a chance to talk this out."

"I'd like that too." Ray reached for her hand. "You've really not been with anyone else?"

Kelly turned her head and her eyes flickered annoyance before she shook her head. "A few dates. A few kisses. But nothing that led to anything else. I couldn't afford to be careless."

Guilt swam in his belly. No, he'd been the careless one when he said he wanted it to all end. God, he had a lot of damage control to do.

CHAPTER 28

*K*elly stood in the shower trying to wake up. Dinner with Ray had been uneventful and quiet. They'd ended up at a sandwich and salad place, shared a brownie after dinner, and went their separate ways.

She wasn't sure what she'd expected, but the calm between them had been nice. And, she had to consider that maybe Ray just didn't want to be alone after his father's funeral, just like he'd said.

Her parents had brought the kids back, and while her father watched a hockey game on the TV, she and her mother had sat at the kitchen table and talked. It had taken nearly an hour, and two cups of tea, before her mother asked about Ray.

"You looked very cozy," her mother mentioned her observations as she sipped from her mug.

Considering the misunderstanding, or so she'd call it, that she and Ray had had over Jeremy's visit, she wondered how much she should tell her mother. They'd jumped feet first into deciding to work on their lost marriage, but then dove right into the mistrust. Yes, they had been very cozy, but strangely enough they always had been.

"We're on very friendly terms." She considered. "Yes, let's call it that."

Her mother smiled from behind her mug. "Friendly terms? I don't think the two of you ever moved on from that even when you got divorced."

"I've been dating someone," Kelly admitted.

The smile that had lit in her mother's eyes faded. "Oh. Who are you seeing?"

Kelly sipped her tea. "I had been seeing Jeremy Cross."

Her mother sipped her tea as well. "I didn't expect that." Her voice had an obvious displeased tone. "You said had been? You're not anymore?"

"I'm going to assume that this has something to do with Ray's father dying, but he says it doesn't," she began and then took a breath. "Ray opened up to me and said he still loves me."

"And what does that have to do with you and Jeremy Cross?" Her mother's voice hardened when she said his name.

"Let's just say I'm not seeing Jeremy anymore because Ray and I are going to take some time to reconsider our marriage."

The smile lit back in her mother's eyes. "You and Ray?"

"I'm not sure it'll work. His jumping to his own decisions still seems to be an issue. But we're going to talk it out."

"I think you'll need to do more than talking, dear," her mother said on a laugh.

Kelly shook her head as she felt the heat rise in her cheeks. "We're going to talk about it," she repeated.

"I'm happy for you."

RACHEL HAD TEXTED KELLY TO REMIND HER ABOUT MARGARITAS and nachos. Of course Kelly was having second thoughts. She wasn't sure what was happening between her and Ray, perhaps it was too early to start hanging out with his friends.

Charlotte, however, was looking forward to the evening, especially since Catherine had mentioned that she was bringing Celia Rose with her. There was no backing out now, Kelly thought.

Connor was more than happy to be going with Ray to Toby's. Kelly had heard all about the huge house in Boulder with its game room, swimming pool, and movie theater. Who wouldn't want to be part of that as often as possible? Though, it did say something about the men that Ray spent time with if they didn't mind him dragging along his six-year-old son. Then again, where Ray had been the exception, now most of them were fathers. Alex had become a father instantly when he'd learned that his ex-girl-friend had had his child and then died in a car accident. And Craig's full nights of sleep were about to end at the beginning of the year. No, Ray wasn't the only outsider in a group of single men anymore.

"Dad's here!" Connor shouted from the top of the stairs before bounding down them so fast it made the pictures on the wall shake.

Kelly walked from the kitchen toward the front door, wiping her hands on a towel, and watching as Connor flung open the door.

The smile on Ray's face warmed her. She hadn't seen him since they'd had dinner after the funeral, but she thought he looked more at ease, though sadness still clouded his eyes.

"Hey, pal," Ray said as he picked Connor up and gave him a tight squeeze. "Are you ready to go?"

"Yup."

"Give me a couple minutes to talk to Mom, okay?"

Connor rolled his eyes and trudged into the living room. He plopped down next to Charlotte and watched whatever she had on the TV.

Kelly folded the towel she had in her hands. "Is everything okay?" she asked as she walked back toward the kitchen.

"Yeah," he said as he pressed his hand to the small of her back and it sent a tingle up her spine.

When they were out of sight of the kids, Ray pulled Kelly to him and wrapped his arms around her. She automatically lifted her arms around his neck and rested her head to his shoulder.

"It's been a really long week," he said softly in her ear. "I needed this."

The thought that she still brought him comfort made Kelly's heart race a little faster.

"Are you sure I'm the one to bring you comfort?" The words were out before she realized it.

Ray eased back and his eyes locked on hers. Lifting his hand to her cheek, he brushed his thumb over her skin. "There are so many things that became clear this past week, and one of them was that you always were my comfort. I was just an idiot."

"Ray…"

"I'm looking forward to dinner tomorrow," he said as he gazed into her eyes.

"We're just going to talk," she reminded him.

"I'm still looking forward to it." He pressed his forehead to hers. "I won't keep him out long."

"Why don't you take him home with you. Make it a full guys' night out. Just have him to school on time."

The smile that eased across his lips squeezed at her heart. "I'd like that."

"Can we go now?" Connor's voice came from behind them and Kelly felt the heat rise in her cheeks.

"One more minute, buddy," Ray said without pulling away from her.

Connor huffed off again and Kelly chuckled. "This has to confuse them."

"Maybe, but it's positive, right? Who doesn't want to see their parents canoodling in the kitchen?"

"I'll see you tomorrow," Kelly said easing back. "For dinner."

When he winked at her, she wondered if she could hold him to just conversation.

CHAPTER 29

When Toby opened the front door, his eyes shifted right to Connor. "Hey buddy. I didn't know you were coming tonight." He held out his hand to shake Connor's.

Ray placed his hand on Connor's shoulder. "I hope you don't mind. We're having a guys' night, and what better place to have it?"

Toby stepped back and let them enter. "Connor is always welcome. We won't make the parties crazy until he's older," Toby joked as Ray narrowed his eyes on him. "I have wings down in the game room. Can I get you something to drink, Ray?"

"I'll just have a soda. Whatever Connor picks."

Connor looked up at him. "I want a Coke."

"Then that's what we'll have."

Craig, Bruce, and Alex were standing around the pool table, each with a cue in their hand. "Hey, Connor is here," Alex shouted. "I call him for my partner."

Ray smiled as Connor's eyes lit up. He picked up a cue and moved in next to Alex who lined him up for his shot.

Toby slid in behind the bar and took two Cokes from the

refrigerator. "Alex said Kelly was going out with the girls tonight?"

Ray nodded. "They invited her. She took Charlotte with her, but she's nervous."

"What's to be nervous about?"

Ray winced as he took the Coke that Toby had poured into a glass with ice. "I think I have her all confused about things, and she doesn't think she fits in with my friends, since she's not sure what will happen between us."

"I thought you guys were going to work on stuff."

"That was until I accused her of going behind my back and keeping her boyfriend."

Toby winced. "Ouch."

"Yeah, ouch."

"What made you do that?"

Leaning in closer to Toby, so that Connor wouldn't hear him, he pursed his lips. "He showed up the other night as I left. She let him into the house and closed the door. So, because I'm me, I accused her of playing us and sleeping with him behind my back, but promising to work on our marriage."

"You were spying on her?" Toby looked genuinely appalled.

"No," Ray said defensively. "I just happened to see him pull up as I pulled away. So I turned back around."

Toby wrinkled up his nose. "And she wasn't sleeping with him behind your back?"

"She hasn't slept with him at all. Or anyone," he confided and then wondered why. "Anyway, she invited him in to break up with him, but I accused her first."

"You're an idiot."

Ray nodded. "And that's why I'm miserably divorced."

"But she went to girls' night. That's a positive, right?"

"And she's making me dinner tomorrow night at the house, and her parents are taking the kids for the weekend."

Toby lifted his bottle of beer and tapped it to Ray's glass. "Here's to a productive weekend."

~

KELLY HELD CHARLOTTE'S HAND AS THEY WALKED INTO THE restaurant, but as soon as Charlotte saw Catherine holding the baby, she pulled away from her mother and ran.

At least she was comfortable with the situation, Kelly thought.

When Rachel noticed her, she fought to scoot out of the booth and stand. When Kelly reached them, Rachel enveloped her in an enormous hug.

Kelly eased back and looked down at Rachel's stomach. "You're nearly ready to go."

"Seriously eight more weeks. I don't think I can handle it. I'm the size of a barn."

"You look beautiful."

"Thank you," Rachel said as she slid back into the booth sitting sideways so she could fit. "Next week we're back to tables. I can't fit in here anymore."

Kelly looked down at her daughter who had given her finger to Celia Rose to play with. "She's beautiful," Kelly said to Catherine as she sat down next to Rachel.

"She is. And luckily she looks like her father. It's always made it a little easier to wrap my head around all of this."

Kelly thought of the story, where the woman Alex had been involved with had had his baby, then she died. But, Alex hadn't known about the baby. Would she have been as brave as Catherine to take on parenting in that situation?

Rachel set her hand on Kelly's knee. "How is Ray? I mean how is he really?"

"He's good."

"And his mom?"

"She's getting along fine. As always, grief sneaks up on you when you least expect it."

Rachel nodded. "Don't I know it."

"I was sorry to hear of your dad's passing. He was a great guy," Kelly offered her condolences.

"He was. I tell ya, when all the guys showed up together, it was if I was right back in high school. And to think, now they're together all the time."

"It means a lot to Ray."

Catherine and Rachel exchanged smiles as Catherine helped Charlotte hold Celia Rose.

"We gotta know. What's going on with you and Ray then?" Rachel finally asked.

"They're going to get married," Charlotte said as she held tightly to the baby.

"Well," Kelly choked out the word. "We talked about working on our marriage. Things are a little strained right now." Suddenly she'd wished she hadn't brought Charlotte. This conversation couldn't go much further.

Rachel nodded, as if maybe she understood Kelly's thoughts.

"He's a good guy."

Kelly nodded. "He is."

"If Craig and I can ever be of assistance, ya know, take the kids or anything, you let us know," Rachel said with a wink.

"Alex and I too. We're here," Catherine offered.

Kelly let out a soft breath. "I appreciate it. We'll see how it goes. My parents are taking the kids for the weekend."

A smile formed on Rachel's lips as she patted Kelly's hand. "Then I expect to see you at the basketball game on Sunday to tell us all about your weekend."

CHAPTER 30

*K*elly stood at the front door and watched as her parents drove away with the kids.

She thought she had put on a good show. There was no reason to tell her mother what she was up to, though Charlotte knew enough that she might say something, but then again, it wasn't as if she were hiding the fact that Ray would be there.

And why was she so nervous she wondered. He wasn't a stranger. This wasn't like having some guy she'd met online come to her house. This was Ray.

Kelly pressed her hands to her stomach as she closed the door and leaned up against it. Dinner. Ray was coming for dinner. They were going to talk, so why was she so nervous to have him there alone?

She knew why—because she still loved him.

Kelly didn't want to rush into anything. After all, the last time they rushed into anything, they got divorced. Getting back together could prove to be equally as harmful if rushed. Dinner, she reminded herself. They were just having dinner.

. . .

Ray had gone home after work, showered, shaved, and changed his clothes. And, in an optimistic move, he packed an overnight bag that was going to stay in his car.

On his way to Kelly's, he picked up a bottle of wine and a bouquet of flowers. He wasn't going in empty handed. He had all intentions of wooing his wife back.

As he walked back to his car, in the parking lot of the store, he heard his name being called. Lifting his head, he noticed Jeremy Cross walking toward him. It was then he realized he had a stranglehold on the flowers.

"Hey, Jeremy," he kept his voice light.

"I assume those are for Kelly, huh?" The man's words were slurred. Had he been drinking already?

As Ray nodded his head, he looked past the man in front of him toward the car in which he'd climbed from. He hoped to hell Jeremy's kids weren't with him. It appeared he was alone, but still a menace to society.

"We're having dinner tonight. I thought it would be a nice surprise."

Jeremy's head continually bobbed as if it had a motor. "Real nice how you swooped on in and reclaimed your property. Funny how you always do that where Kelly is concerned."

"Hey, man, no hard feelings. I know we've been in this position before, but Kelly was my wife for a long time. We have two great kids, and our divorce was a mistake. I'm ready to right that wrong."

The cackle that Jeremy let out had Ray pulling open his car door with all intentions of zipping out of that parking lot. The man in front of him, usually decent and understanding, had a hint of madness in his eyes now, fueled by liquor.

Ray set the bottle and the flowers in the seat and turned back to tell Jeremy goodbye. Instead, as he turned, Jeremy's fist smashed right into Ray's cheek knocking him back against the car.

Before Ray could regain his balance, Jeremy landed two more punches—one to his stomach and another to his face.

Luckily Jeremy staggered then, enough that Ray, his vision now compromised, could push him back and into the arms of the security guard that had come rushing toward them.

As the guard assessed the situation, and a police officer pulled up behind Ray's car, Ray leaned against the open door and tried to gain his focus. That was a cheap shot, he thought as he pressed his fingers to his throbbing cheek.

They'd done that once before, and again, it was over Kelly's honor. What in the world had she been thinking letting the lunatic back into her life?

THE TEARS THAT ROLLED DOWN HER FACE WERE UNATTENDED TO. Kelly's body was numb from anger. She blew out the stubs of the candles that had been burning for hours.

Only because she was practical, she filled containers with the food she'd made and put it in the refrigerator.

She couldn't believe that Ray had never showed up—nor had he called.

Obviously something else was more important, or he'd changed his mind. Maybe it was all cemented in his grief, and maybe he hadn't been interested in her at all.

And it would be just petty enough of him to make her think there had been a chance for them, and she'd broken everything off with Jeremy.

Not that anything was going to come about with Jeremy, but for the brief moment he was in her life again, it was nice to be wanted.

Kelly turned off the lights and headed upstairs. She washed her tear-streaked face, slipped into her pajamas, and tied her hair up on top of her head.

As she pulled back the sheets on the bed, she heard the knocking at the door. Immediately her hands began to shake, and she stood there contemplating what she was going to do.

He deserved to stand there and knock all night. There was no reason she needed to let him into the house after he stood her up.

Then again, would it be satisfying to give him a piece of her mind?

With that thought, Kelly hurried down the stairs and pulled open the door.

She sucked in a breath to let the barrage of angry words flow, but she noticed his face in the shadows.

His cheek was cut and his eye was swollen nearly shut. There was blood in the corner of his mouth.

In his hands he carried a bottle of wine and wilted flowers.

"What in the world happened to you?" she asked as she pulled him into the house and turned on the light.

He winced. "I had a little altercation in the parking lot earlier when I went to pick up the wine." Looking down at the flowers in his hand, he handed them to her. "These are for you. They could use a little water."

Kelly took the flowers he offered, but kept her eyes on him. "Ray, who did this?"

"Is it important? What matters is that I'm here. We have a lot to discuss."

"You look like shit."

"I feel like shit."

The tears were back and she wanted to pull him in, but she didn't dare. "Seriously, Ray. Who did this to you?"

"Let's just say, Jeremy might not be taking your breakup so well."

CHAPTER 31

*K*elly took Ray's hand and pulled him into the kitchen. She was in caretaker mode now. She pulled open the freezer and took out a bag of frozen peas. Then she wrapped the bag in a towel, before guiding Ray to sit down and press the bag to his eye.

She went on to boil water in the kettle, set out mugs, find tea bags, and lastly pull out the containers of food she'd stored.

All the while Ray watched her fidget in the kitchen trying to get a grip on what had happened to him. Watching her move about only made her more endearing.

When the kettle whistled, she poured water into the mugs, and added tea bags. And as she turned to set his mug in front of him, all he could do was smile up at her, the bag of peas pressed against his eye.

"Why are you grinning like that?" she asked, obviously frazzled to her last nerve.

"Because you're beautiful buzzing around here like this."

"I'm mad, Ray. I'm shaking mad."

"I see that. At least I'm hoping you're not shaking mad at me now."

Kelly stopped and wrapped her arms around herself. "I was mad at you. I had no idea…"

"How could you have?"

"You should have called."

"I was busy."

"Getting your ass kicked?"

The very comment had them both chuckle, and the air had diffused a bit from the strain that had filled it.

"We had to file a report, because the security at the store got involved. Then they took me to the urgent care to get my cheek stitched up, and the back of my head where I hit the car," he said as he lifted his hand to touch those stitches too.

"I can't believe he did that," Kelly let out a sob and covered her mouth with her hand.

"I can. We did it before, a decade ago. Last time we were both drunk. This time it was only him."

Her eyes went wide. "You beat each other up?"

"Yeah, only that time, I got in a few licks. This time, he blind-sided me."

"I didn't know you'd done this before."

Ray set the peas on the table and reached for her hand, pulling her down onto his lap. "You're a catch, Kel. And I've been lucky enough to be the recipient of your love all this time. Only, I was too stupid to hold on to it. I don't hold this against him. Hell, when I found out you were seeing him again, I'd considered doing the same thing."

"You're stupid."

"I'm not arguing that." He smiled up into her eyes, resting his hand on her cheek. "I'm sorry I wasn't here for dinner. It smells good in here."

"I was so mad at you."

"And you should be," he admitted. "But now you know why I wasn't here. I never would have stood you up."

"Now what? Are you hungry?"

He gave it some thought. "I think I am."

"I'll warm it up. You sit here. Put that bag back on your eye."

As she lifted to leave his lap, he pulled her back down. "I need one more thing," he said.

"What?"

"Kiss me, Kel. Kiss me and make the pain go away."

KELLY STUDIED HIS FACE. THE CUT ON HIS CHEEK AND HIS SWOLLEN eye made her stomach ache.

She unwrapped the towel from the peas and licked the corner. Gently, she brushed it over the corner of his mouth to wipe away the blood.

Her lip trembled as she studied him. There was no reason to think that they needed just a night to talk, and she'd known that since the moment he'd kissed her in the parking lot of his office.

Setting the towel on the table, she stood, readjusted, and now straddled Ray. His eyes had gone wide for a moment, but then a smile settled on his lips. Resting her hand on his unaffected cheek, Kelly hesitated for a moment as Ray steadied his hands on her hips, causing a tingle to zip up her spine..

"This is it, isn't it?" she asked.

"What's that?"

"I was trying to be strong and decent," she giggled. "I swore all I wanted to do tonight was talk to you."

"I'm right here, Kel. Let's talk."

She shook her head. "I don't want to talk."

His fingers gripped her tighter, and from beneath her, she could feel that he would understand what she was about to say.

"I've missed you, Ray."

He licked his lips. "I haven't gone anywhere."

Oh, he was playing it cool. Kelly lowered her lips until they brushed his. "I want you back."

"I'm glad to hear it."

"I want to spend the weekend with you. I don't want to get dressed. I don't want to be seen. I just want to wrap myself around you and keep you to myself."

He smiled against her lips. "You'll get no argument from me."

"I'm not against having sex in the kitchen, right here in this chair, but you look a bit uncomfortable."

That made him chuckle and he eased his head back to look at her. "When did you get so bold?"

"When I let you walk out the door and starved myself of any pleasure for two years."

He nodded slowly. "So this is just sex? Feed a need?"

"No, Ray. This is love," she said surely and watched as his eyes went moist. "I should have fought for you. Especially since there wasn't another woman or anything beyond pettiness that kept us apart. I should have fought."

"You love me?"

"I have always loved you."

He lifted his hands to cup her cheeks. "Say it, Kel. Tell me."

Covering his hands on her cheeks, she locked eyes with him. "I love you."

"I love you too."

"Will you take me to bed?"

Ray pulled her to him, opening his mouth to her, and causing her head to spin with the kiss he offered.

When he eased back, he pressed his forehead to hers. "Lead the way."

CHAPTER 32

*A*gain, because it was responsible, Kelly tossed the containers of food back into the refrigerator and turned off the lights as she held tightly to Ray's hand leading him through the house.

Her heart raced. They'd done this same routine hundreds of times, before and after kids. Walking up the stairs where pictures of their family lined the walls, Kelly felt the warmth of pride rise in her chest. No other man had taken this same walk with her—not a one.

She could hear him breathing behind her. Was his heart racing? Did he understand the significance of this walk?

As soon as she crossed the threshold into her bedroom, Ray kicked the door closed, pulled her back to him, and pushed her up against the door.

"That was a long walk, Kel," he said pressing his body hard against hers, his lips moving to her neck.

Kelly sucked in a breath, raising her arms around Ray's neck, as he feasted on hers.

It had been so long since the energy that buzzed through her had awoken. Even the nights she'd spent kissing Jeremy were nothing in comparison to Ray running his tongue over her skin.

His fingers skimmed under the hem of her tank top, and then his hands pressed against her stomach. Again, she sucked in a breath.

Her stomach wasn't taut and flat. There were marks that crossed it and a softness to it that she'd never embraced. But when Ray's hands moved over her bare skin, the energy that zipped through her made her forget what hid in the dark.

Kelly raked her fingers into his hair as she gasped for air beneath him. Ray's hands had moved to her ribs, and then to her breasts where his thumbs brushed against alert nipples.

Her entire body quaked beneath his touch.

Ray lifted the thin fabric up and over her head, and replaced his hands with his mouth, which led Kelly to let out a moan.

Moving his mouth back to hers, he made quick work of pulling off her shorts and taking the band out of her hair so that her hair fell over her shoulders.

"You're so beautiful, Kel."

She chuckled. "You can't see me in the dark."

"I don't have to. I know every inch of this body—better than I know my own." His hands wandered to her shoulder. "Tree branch scar from when you were eight."

Kelly let out a breath as he traveled kisses from her collar, between her breasts, over her stomach, and down her thigh to her knee. "Knee surgery after a missed cheer landing tore your ACL."

Again his kisses wandered upward, stopping at her soft belly. Ray held his hands there, and she could feel the stirring of energy beneath his fingertips.

"This is a beautiful road map to parenthood." He kissed her skin. "Connor." He kissed her belly again. "Charlotte."

Now the shudder of energy was caught in a gentle sob, and

Ray rose, gathering her in his arms and pressing a warm kiss to her mouth.

"Don't cry," he said, brushing his tongue over her bottom lip.

"I can't help it. I haven't been touched like this in years. And I'm a little self-conscious of my stomach," she laughed.

"I created those," Ray admitted as he let his hand linger on her soft belly. "These are our scars. I'm so freaking proud of them."

"You are?"

"I am, Kel. I love you."

She let the sob diminish on a breath. "I love you too. I never did stop."

"I'm so happy to hear you say that."

RAY HOISTED KELLY TO HIS HIPS, FEELING HER WARMTH PRESSED against his belly. This wasn't about sex, and he needed to make sure she understood that, but at the same time, he wanted to please her so she'd never forget again.

With her arms wrapped tightly around his neck, Ray cupped her bottom in his hands as he walked them toward the bed. Laying her down, he studied her in the sliver of moonlight that lit the bed.

"You're beautiful," he said again.

"Ray…"

He pressed a finger to her lips. "I don't want you to ever forget this night."

"I won't," she promised on an airy breath, her hands now gripping his shirt. But he took her hands in his. "You first," he said as he placed his hands on her shoulders and eased her back on the bed.

She trembled beneath him as he took her mouth and stirred up the heat between them.

She deserved to feel special tonight, he thought as he began pressing kisses to her goose-bumped skin. Trailing over her with his tongue, he appreciated the taste of her. Her body shook under his touch, and he appreciated the motion. Again, his hands glided over scars she saw as imperfections, and he appreciated them even more than he ever had.

How had he let this perfect woman out of his grasp? How had he been so selfish to think it had gotten so hard he couldn't cope? Not one day had passed since he'd said those words to her, *I want a divorce*, that he hadn't regretted them.

"Ray," her voice was soft as her hands splayed out on his shoulders. "Are you okay?"

He shimmied back up her body, easing himself on top of her. "I'm so sorry, Kel."

She sucked in a breath. "For what?" Her words trembled as much as her body did.

"For letting you go. I caused this. Not for anyone else, or even for a better opportunity. I was selfish."

"But you're here now." She brushed her hand over his hair. "We can do this. Not the sex, but the marriage. We can do it."

"Marry me again, Kel," the words shot from his mouth, and as she took a breath, he pressed his fingers to her lips. "Wait. Don't say anything. I don't want this to be a proposal. I got caught up in it."

"But, Ray…"

"No," he brushed his lips against hers again. "I'm not going to bring it up again the rest of the weekend. I don't want you to either. Let's assume that's where we're going, but let's not think about it. I have you all weekend to myself. I want to kiss you, hold you, sleep in your arms. I want to make breakfast with you in our kitchen, and have sex with you in every room of this house," he said and she laughed beneath him. "We'll talk about the marriage thing when the kids are here and they can have a say. It's not only us now, and I get that. I get that so much more than I did when I walked away."

Kelly cupped his face in her hands, and he fought the wince from the pain to his cheek.

"I love you, Ray. Don't wait too long for me to give you an answer to the question you're going to ask me again."

She pulled him down to her mouth and took them both under with a deep kiss, stirring the heat between them again.

"Now," he said easing away from her. "I'm going to worship this body that I love. Close your eyes and enjoy."

CHAPTER 33

*R*ay lay looking up at the ceiling, his breath coming in only pants. His head and cheek throbbed, but it had been worth it. For the past three hours, he'd worshiped Kelly's body, and she'd reciprocated.

There had been a lot of pleasure in knowing he'd been the last man to please her, and he'd made sure to do the same again. Mixed with that, there was guilt that swam in his belly. In time they'd talk about it. She might not have been with anyone since they'd parted, but he couldn't say the same, and he wasn't proud of it.

In fact, the thought, which had come to him as Kelly had wrapped her mouth around him, had nearly made him sick. There had been two more, one night each, and his chest tightened when he thought about them.

Seriously, he could go on and she'd never know. But in time she'd ask, he had. God, why hadn't she run out and done the same thing?

Because she was secure in who she was, and as she'd said to him before, she couldn't risk it.

Their children came first to her, and they always had, and Ray knew that. So why had they slipped his mind on those two occasions? Because he wasn't married to their mother, that's why. He had to remember, he did nothing wrong, but sweaty from the best sex he'd ever had in his life, they haunted him now.

Kelly's hand came to his heaving chest. "It's been a long time since we made a marathon of this," she laughed as she rested her head on his shoulder. "But we used to do that a lot, until the kids came along."

"Yeah, but you have to admit, the trade off was worth it."

"You're right." She rolled and pressed her hands on his chest, lifting to look at him in the shadows. "Do you remember we used to talk about four kids?"

Ray reached up and tucked a strand of hair behind her ear. "I remember."

"I think we'd even named them all."

He chuckled. "We did, and if I'm not mistaken, when the time came, we didn't use any of the names we'd chosen."

Kelly laughed and eased down beside him, his arm now wrapped around her. "You're right. Those were happy times," she said on a sigh, but neither of them mentioned what came after that.

"What time is it?" Ray whispered.

Kelly shifted, picked up her phone and looked at the time. "Three-thirty."

Ray gently ran circles over her shoulder with his fingertips. "I'm exhausted, but I'm starving."

"So am I," Kelly admitted. "I can go down and warm up dinner. Or, I could make us some sandwiches."

Ray shook his head. "This weekend is about adventure, right?"

Kelly laughed. "What did you have in mind?"

Ray rolled so that he was on top of her looking down. "All night sex requires something more hearty. Let's get dressed and head to IHOP."

Kelly laughed harder. "You're joking, right?"

"Not in the least. Let's go have a big stack of pancakes, and maybe on the drive home we could find a place to watch the sun come up."

"We're going to be exhausted tomorrow—today."

"Your parents have the kids. We're responsibility-free, so to speak."

Kelly gazed up at him, and he knew he'd never—ever spend another night without her wrapped around him.

"Suddenly, I do have a hankering for some pancakes."

THEY SAT IN THE EARLY MORNING, NOVEMBER COLD, ON THE STEPS at Red Rocks Amphitheater, after filling up on coffee and pancakes, and watched as the sky began to change into brilliant hues of pinks and oranges.

They cuddled under a quilt that Ray's grandmother had made them for their wedding, and which Kelly used daily on the back of the couch.

Kelly rested her head to Ray's shoulder, and he wrapped his arm around her shoulder.

"We should do this every year. We could make it an anniversary of sorts," he suggested.

"I'd like that."

"We could call it, the anniversary of when Ray got his head out of his ass."

Kelly chuckled and eased back to look at him. She gently lifted her fingers to his stitched up cheek. "Does that hurt?"

"Smiling makes it hurt, but I can't stop, so…"

"I can't believe he punched you."

"I can," Ray said, taking her hand and holding it in hers. "You're worth fighting for. And I know that now from first-hand experience. I should have fought harder before giving it all up."

Kelly brushed a gentle kiss to his lips. "Can we have Thanksgiving together? It's your week, and I'm sure your mother wants to have some normality for Thanksgiving. My parents are heading to my brother's, since they came here for the funeral and all. Maybe we can just have something simple at the house and call it Thanksgiving."

"You know that Mom will want you at her house for dinner."

"I don't know that, but I want to be together at some point during the day."

Ray tucked the blanket around her tighter. "We're together, Kel. This is it. We do it all together now. No more my house or your house—my week or your week. We're a family."

"I thought we were going to wait until we talked to the kids."

Ray snickered. "We are, and I'd be very disappointed after all of this if you turned me away."

"But you don't want me to answer that question you asked in bed?"

"No. Save your answer."

Kelly eased against him. "All of this has been such a waste of time. I mean, the money we spent to end something that should have just been worked on, only to end up right here, and to have never been with other people, it seems so wasteful."

Ray's breath froze in his lungs, and it wasn't due to the cold around them. He needed to come clean to her, but he wanted to know they were committed first.

CHAPTER 34

*K*elly sipped the strong coffee in the paper cup and held the muffin in her hand. She wasn't sure how she was going to make it through the day. Ray drove toward the YMCA for his weekly basketball game with his teammates from college, and she wondered where he'd gotten his energy.

"Maybe I can just sleep in the car while you play," she suggested as she rested her head back against the seat and closed her eyes.

"Rachel and Catherine are expecting you. You're part of the clique now."

Kelly rolled her head to the side. "They're going to want sexy details."

"It's the perfect week for you to give them," he said laughing. "The kids aren't around to hear them."

"I'd be so embarrassed if they heard about all the things we did this weekend."

"Don't think I don't intend to rush home after, too. I only have a few more hours alone with you, and I plan to make the most of it."

Kelly laughed and took another drink of her coffee.

This was how it should always be, she thought.

WHEN THEY WALKED INTO THE GYM, IT WAS CRAIG WHO CAME AT them first.

"Now this is a sight for sore eyes," he said wrapping his arms around Kelly and planting a kiss on her cheek. "I'm so happy to see you drag this loser around. He needs someone like you in his life." Craig studied the stitches on Ray's face. "A caretaker, that is."

Kelly laughed. "Well, it appears that's just what he has."

Craig settled his eyes on her. "Really? You two worked it out?"

"I think we have. We're going to talk to the kids first," she said and Craig pulled her in to hug her.

Of all the men he'd played basketball with, it had been Craig Turner that that been in their lives as a married couple, and the only one of the teammates who had been at their wedding. Having grown up with Ray, they had a different relationship, and Kelly envied that. But, she was openminded enough to think that the two women who added her to their plans for nachos and margaritas could be those kinds of friends to her too.

When Craig released her, she walked toward the bleachers and took a seat next to Rachel and Catherine. As Kelly brushed her hand over Celia Rose's hair, Catherine shifted her.

"Here, you feed her," she said handing her the baby and the bottle. "I'll bet you need a baby fix."

Kelly wondered if the heat that had filled her cheeks actually pinked on her face as she took the baby. "I've had my babies," she said.

Catherine shook her head. "Hell, you're still young. Besides, it could be a trifecta," she said at the same time Alex said something to Ray that warranted a slap to the back.

"What do you mean?"

Catherine exchanged smiles with Rachel, who rubbed her

enlarged belly. "Alex and I are going to have another baby. I'm pregnant," Catherine beamed.

Noticing that Celia Rose had fallen asleep, yet still sucked on the bottle, Kelly contained her excitement for her new friend, and kept her voice low. "That's very exciting. Congratulations."

"Thanks. It's new—really new. I took a test a few days ago, and then made the doctor run one too. We're only three weeks in, and I know everyone says not to say anything, you know, in case something goes wrong. But, I can't help myself."

Kelly laughed. "I'm very happy for you," she said and looked up to see that Ray was watching her with Celia Rose.

Was it in the stars for them, she wondered? When Ray smiled at her, she knew Alex had shared the same news with him that Catherine had shared with her. And seeing her holding the baby probably was making him wonder the same things she was.

Kelly let out a soft breath as she looked down at the sleeping baby in her arms. It was all moving too fast, but then again, their breakup had happened that fast as well. Obviously that had been a mistake. Was considering moving forward a mistake too?

Celia Rose found her thumb as she sleep, sucking on it, and Kelly swallowed hard as emotions rose. It wasn't a mistake. She loved Ray. She loved her family. They should all be together, it was bigger than the two of them.

And, she batted away tears that threatened, if it was in the stars, maybe there would be another baby for them. She'd be okay with that.

THEY HELD HANDS IN THE CAR AS THEY DROVE HOME, RAY RIPE from the game that had him and his pals playing for nearly two hours.

He shifted a glance toward Kelly, who smiled as she watched the scenery pass by.

"You're a million miles away," he said, running his thumb over her knuckles.

"Deep in thought I guess."

"That's some news, huh? Catherine and Alex?"

"I'm happy for them. I didn't even mention just how tired they're going to be with babies only fifteen months apart. No parent appreciates that. You just figure it out."

"We did okay."

"We were potty training Connor before Charlotte showed up. It was a little different," she reminded him.

"But if I remember correctly, when she arrived, he regressed."

That caused Kelly to laugh and roll her head to look at him. "You're right. We did okay, considering."

"You looked beautiful and content holding Celia Rose."

"It's sad that her mother died, but she's a lucky little girl to have Catherine."

"She is. And it wasn't easy. Catherine had her doubts. She nearly called it all off."

"Now that we're back together, I can't imagine anything that would make me call it off again. I know so much now."

Ray gave her hand a squeeze and lifted her fingers to his lips.

He thought about the fights they would still have, they were bound to come along. He'd promised Connor that he'd try not fighting with her, and if they did, they'd work it out.

He agreed with her, he decided, as he pulled the car into the driveway. He couldn't imagine them not being together again, too.

CHAPTER 35

*K*elly had been up since five baking rolls, making pies, and trying to perfect her mother's stuffing.

They had decided to keep the living arrangements the same until the holiday break, as to not confuse the kids, who were already confused by their parents' affection for each other.

Clara had begged Kelly to join them for Thanksgiving, and she wasn't sure if it was genuine or coaxed, though she assumed Clara did want her there.

They'd be eating early, as they always did at Clara's house. And now with Kelly's parents not living nearby, they no longer needed to plan for multiple Thanksgiving dinners in one day.

As she slid the pies in the oven, her phone rang and she heard her children's voices singing good morning to her. It put a lightness in her chest as they each wished her good morning, and then scurried off to do other things. When Ray took over the call, the lightness stayed.

"I can't wait to see you," he said.

"You saw me last night at dinner."

"Proof that I just can't wait until Christmas. I don't want to watch you drive away."

"It's best for them right now. Little bits."

"I suppose. But I'd rather have you in my arms at night so I can do what we did over the weekend whenever I want."

Kelly felt the blush of heat move over her skin. "They'd better not be within earshot of you."

"Totally preoccupied with other things. We'll head out of here in about a half hour and come pick you up."

Kelly blew a strand of hair from her face. "I'll go get myself ready. I'm nervous about this, you know."

"Don't be. It's not new, Kel. You've spent the better part of a month with my mother. She adores you. Remember, she told you."

That was true. "I'll see you soon."

~

KELLY HAD DECORATED FOR CHRISTMAS, THE FRIDAY AFTER Thanksgiving. Taking his week seriously, Ray had taken the kids to work with him, and Kelly felt strangely freed.

She decorated, planned out Christmas lists for the kids, and made grocery lists for baking. It had been a long time since she'd wanted to celebrate, but this year was special. This year she'd get her family back.

Kelly took in a deep breath as she thought about it. They hadn't committed, well, not fully as in her accepting the proposal he'd offered. They'd agreed to wait. But in her heart she knew that they'd be planning a wedding soon.

A wedding. Should they just elope? No, the kids needed to be involved. They could do a private ceremony, but then Ray would want his friends, and even though her friend base was much smaller, she'd want them there too. Was it appropriate to have a big second wedding? Should they keep it small?

Kelly laughed at herself and went back to making her lists. They'd figure it out together.

Nachos and Non-Alcoholic delights? The text message flashed on her phone from Rachel.

On Thursday? she replied.

Tonight. We know Ray has the kids, and we missed girls' night yesterday. Are you in?

Kelly thought about the invitation. She supposed her friend base had grown quite a bit in the past month. All of Ray's friends, and their wives, had become very important and special to her.

She ran her fingers over the screen, *I'll be there.*

THEY OCCUPIED A TABLE NEAR THE BAR, AND RACHEL USED THE extra chair to put her feet up on.

"I don't think you'll make your due date," Kelly told her. "You look much further along."

"Thank you," Rachel said. "I keep saying that, but with technology what it is, they're fairly sure I'm right on track. I just look enormous."

They all laughed at that.

Kelly turned her attention to the newest mother, who didn't have her child with her this time. "How are you feeling?"

"I'm doing okay. Smells are starting to get to me. As in, we may need to find somewhere else to have girls' night next week," she admitted.

"Come to my house. I'll put out a charcuterie board, we can watch some horrible eighties flick, and we can gossip all night with our feet up." There was a giddiness to her voice as she invited them.

Rachel nodded. "I'm in. A comfy place to kick up my feet sounds good to me."

Kelly turned to Catherine. "My bathroom will be clean for your newly constant use," she teased. "And I'll make sure to air everything out before you get there."

"No heavy candles. I hate that I can't have that around me."

Kelly pulled a chip from the plate. "I totally understand. And each pregnancy is different too. I couldn't do poultry with Connor and loved fish. With Charlotte if it had a face, it made me sick. I mean a face before it was set on my plate."

Rachel laughed. "I don't think there is anything I don't want. I've eaten everything and that's probably why I'm the size of a house."

Catherine put her hand into the center of the table. "Let's take an oath. As soon as we are done being pregnant, we'll meet on Thursdays for yoga."

Rachel and Kelly both placed their hands over Catherine's and agreed. Though Kelly didn't know what was in store for her and Ray. They'd talked about it, but she was happy with her kids. Maybe it was good to just love them forever and move forward.

Then again, as she looked at Rachel pressing her hand to a place on her belly where the baby was practicing his or her field goal kicks, and Catherine excused herself to the bathroom, she missed all of the horrors of being pregnant.

Maybe it was worth thinking about just a little more.

CHAPTER 36

*K*elly wiped her hand over her brow and looked at the plate of cookies on her desk. The last day before winter break, and every student in her class must have brought her cookies or chocolates for Christmas. She had thought it was a great thing, seeing as her Starbucks account was padded for years after last Christmas, teacher appreciation, her birthday, and end of year gifts from the previous school year.

She'd already partaken of the candy that the room-parents had brought as part of a game they'd put together. There was a plate of cookies missing, because after having forgotten breakfast, she'd eaten them during recess and lunch break. Now, she pressed her hand to her unsettled stomach and thought of making a nice salad for dinner.

After the girls' night at her house, they had decided to postpone other nights until after the new year, or Kelly thought she could have pawned off some of the cookies on her expectant mommy friends. Maybe she still could, she humored. She had gifts for both Rachel and Catherine. A drop by might just be in order.

When the door to her classroom opened, Ray walked in with

two very happy kids who were more than ready to have a break from school for the next few weeks. He had taken the afternoon off to help in Connor's classroom with the party, and he looked equally as excited that the day had concluded.

"Mommy," Charlotte bounded toward her holding a plate in her hand. "We decorated gingerbread men. Look at mine."

"Sweetheart, he's perfect."

"Do you think I should leave him out for Santa? Maybe he likes gingerbread and Christmas Eve is only two days away."

Kelly thought of what would really happen to the cookie and she drew in her brows. "Maybe you can draw him a picture of your cookie. We're going to make special Santa cookies tomorrow."

Charlotte nodded as Connor handed her a card. "This is from my teacher. It's just a dumb Christmas card. She gave one to everyone and said to give it to our parents."

Kelly took the card and laughed at the lack of sentiment her son had.

As Connor followed Charlotte to draw on the board, Ray moved in and wrapped an arm around her. "Are you okay? Your face is red."

"I've eaten so many cookies, I think I'm going to burst."

"The more cookies, the more of you there is to love," he said and she growled.

"I don't like that at all."

He looked over his shoulder at the kids drawing at the board. "Let's tell them tonight."

"Ray, we need to decide what we're going to tell them."

"I guess, but we said when school was out. Well, school is out, and I'd really like to sleep in your bed tonight."

"I'd really like that too."

. . .

CLARA JOINED THEM FOR DINNER, AT KELLY'S, AND THOUGH CLARA knew what they were working on, it didn't help settle Kelly's cookie bellyache.

"This was a nice treat," Clara said as Charlotte climbed up into her grandmother's lap. "Dinner time is hard when your partner isn't there to eat with you anymore."

Ray rested his hand on his mother's. "You always have a chair at our table," he said and Kelly looked at both of their children to see if that registered with them or not. But neither of them seemed to have understood his reference.

"I appreciate that. It's all part of the greater plan. When you get married and you love someone unconditionally, you know that one of you will be alone again. You just never know when or which one."

The ache in Kelly's stomach tightened. "Excuse me," she said as she headed up the stairs to her bedroom. She was sure those Christmas cookies were coming back up, especially after the heavy dinner she'd just eaten, and the sentimental aching her mother-in-law was enduring.

She closed her bedroom door and her bathroom door, and as she predicted, her stomach rejected the contents.

It was no surprise that only a moment later Ray was standing at the door tapping on it before he pushed it open.

"Are you okay?" he asked handing her the hand towel.

"Do you know how many cookies I ate today? Seriously, a bakers two dozen," she laughed as she sat back against the cool wall and wiped her mouth.

"That's all that's wrong?"

Kelly lifted her brows and looked at him. "I get sick every year around Christmas. The stress of getting through the semester, the testing, the parties, and the kids' rambunctiousness before Christmas, it always wears me down. Add a few dozen cookies and a heavy dinner, yeah, I'm just fine," she laughed.

"I think it just gave me license to stay the night."

Kelly shook her head. "You're determined, aren't you?"

"Kel, they know we love each other."

"But we're not married."

He let out a groan. "Are you going to make me wait until we're married to sleep in your bed with them here?"

"No. I just don't want to confuse them more."

"Seriously, their parents love them and love each other. Yeah, for most of their memorable life, we haven't lived together, but they knew we loved each other. They're not dumb."

"I didn't say they were."

"I just think they're rational enough to accept it."

She felt another wave of cookies coming up and she shooed Ray out the door and kicked the door closed before she hurled into the toilet one more time.

After flushing the toilet, she rested her back to the wall again, and wiped her mouth. Perhaps it wasn't such a horrible idea. It would be really nice to have him around all night, especially if she was coming down with something more than a sugar overload.

CHAPTER 37

"*D*o you think she'll be okay," Clara asked as she buttoned up her coat and pulled on her gloves. "I worry about her."

"She's fine, Mom. Every kid in her class gave her plates of cookies, and she partook in too many. Besides, she's run down. This time of year is extra busy for teachers who are parents."

"I know. I know." Clara looked into the other room where the kids sat on the couch and watched a movie. "Where are you with getting back together? Charlotte hasn't said much and she'd have told me if her parents were getting married."

Ray chuckled. "We wanted to keep things as normal as possible until Christmas. So we've kept our weeks with the kids, only we eat dinner as a family in whichever home has the kids. We know they understand it, but we don't want to confuse them. Charlotte really doesn't remember us ever living together, and the morning Dad died, well, they caught us in bed together—sleeping," he added. "I wanted her comfort, and she'd been asleep, so I asked her to stay right there."

"And they were confused?"

"They assumed it meant we were married again. But I have

plans," he whispered. "Christmas morning, I'm going to propose with a ring. I'm going to have the kids help me out with it."

He saw the glimmer of a tear in his mother's eye. "That's very romantic."

"I figure I get a second chance, I have to make it count, right? I can't let her go again."

His mother pressed a hand to his cheek, running her thumb over the new scar. "She's a lucky woman. I can't wait to hear all about it."

Ray pulled on his own coat and walked his mother to her car. When she was strapped in, he leaned in and kissed his mother's cheek. "Drive safe and text me when you get home. I love you."

"I love you too, son."

Ray stood in the driveway until his mother was out of sight, then he went back into the house, pulled off his coat, and checked on the kids after throwing it in the chair.

"Are you leaving, Dad?" Connor asked, and Charlotte looked up at him with questioning eyes.

"I don't think so. Mom isn't feeling too well. Would you guys be okay if I stay here tonight, with Mommy?"

Connor shrugged but Charlotte kept an eye on him. "Sammy says Mommy is going to marry you," she informed him and he thought it wildly interesting that Sammy always had the answers to his life.

"We're talking about that."

"I want you to marry Mommy."

The smile tugged at his cheeks and his heart swelled in his chest. "I want to marry Mommy too. I'm going to go check on her, and I'll be back down to get you two ready for bed."

Connor groaned. "It's vacation. Can't we stay up later?"

"Buddy, I still have to work tomorrow. How about I ask Mommy if you can have a pajama day."

"Okay, and stay up?"

"No."

Connor sunk down into his seat and crossed his arms.

Ray turned away as to not let his very sensitive son see him laughing.

When he reached the bedroom, he noticed the flicker of the TV light from under the door. Gently he pushed open the door, stepped in, and closed it behind him.

"You're looking much better," he said with a raised brow as he looked at Kelly propped up on the bed watching a movie.

"Seems to have passed. I feel just fine. See, I told you I ate too many cookies."

"Do you think you could at least pretend to be sick? I have permission to have a sleepover to take care of you," he offered as he moved toward the bed and laid down next to her.

"You have permission, huh?"

"I do. They think it's a fine idea. And, I have some news."

She laughed as she scooted closer to him. "What kind of news."

"It appears that Sammy says we're getting married."

Kelly covered her mouth to stifle a further laugh. "You don't say. Sammy is very wise in my affairs."

"That's what I was thinking. I'm thinking of asking for some stock insight. I mean the kid knows a lot."

Kelly pushed him back and straddled him. Her eyes were still dark from having gotten sick, but otherwise she radiated in the flicker of the TV.

Ray tucked his hands under the thin fabric of her tank top and cupped her breasts.

"Maybe we should have you sleep on the couch," Kelly teased as she rocked back on him, raising her brows as she felt him against her.

"I think I need to be very—very close to you in case you *need* me."

Kelly bit down on her lip. "Connor asked to stay up late, didn't he?"

Ray's thumb brushed over her taut nipples and he nodded. "I said I'd ask if he could have a pajama day tomorrow in lieu of a later bedtime."

Kelly rolled from him, and he let out a groan. She stood, walked to the door, and locked it. As she walked back to the bed, she let her shorts fall, and lifted the tank top up and over her head, letting it fall to the floor too.

"Maybe they can stay up for a few minutes," she said as she straddled him again. "But, mister, you're going to have to be very quiet. You're supposed to be taking care of me in my fragile state."

Ray gripped her hips, rolled her to her back, and hovered over her. "Oh, I'll take care of you in your fragile state," he teased as he pressed a kiss to her belly. "So, you'd better be very quiet."

CHAPTER 38

*R*ay hurried through the house to gather his things. He was already late, but he'd texted Catherine and let her know.

Kelly stood in the kitchen with a travel coffee mug in her hand smiling at him, knowing he still had to go by his house to change his clothes. "Maybe you'd better just bring some clothes over and leave them," she said as she watched him shrug on his coat, his hair still damp from the shower they'd shared.

"Why don't I just move my stuff back in? Christmas is in two days." He took the mug from her, set it on the counter, and wrapped her up in his arms. "It's time, Kel. We're in this now."

Lifting her arms around his neck, she rested her head to his chest. "I guess you're right. Why am I so nervous?"

"It's a big step, and we decided on this in less than a month. I get it."

"I know it's going to work out."

"It will." He kissed her forehead, reached for the coffee mug, and stepped back. "What are your plans?"

"We're supposed to make cookies," she said laughing, looking at the plates of cookies she had sitting on the table from her students. "I think maybe we'll only make Santa's cookies. And, even though we decided against nachos and margaritas with the girls, we were going to meet at Catherine's and exchange gifts tonight. We were going to do it here, but she thought she'd be more comfortable at her house. I won't be but an hour or so."

"I'm okay to come back here then, I assume?"

She moved to him again and pressed a warm, lingering kiss to his lips. "Bring your stuff, Ray. You're right. It's time."

HE LET OUT A BREATH, SET HIS MUG DOWN, AGAIN, AND HELD Kelly close. Why had he ever walked away from this?

"You should go back to bed for a little bit. You look tired," he said as he kissed her cheek.

"I'm a working mother. I always look tired."

No, this was different, he thought. "Still, you look like you could use some rest. It's good that you have a few weeks off."

Ray started for the door and she followed. "I guess I don't know your plans. Do you get any time off?"

He opened the door, turned, and grinned. "We're taking off Christmas Eve tomorrow and Christmas, and New Year's Eve and New Year's Day."

She wrinkled up her nose. "That's not a lot."

"Contracts have to be fulfilled and buildings need to go up." He brushed one more kiss across her lips. "Call me if you need me, especially if you're not feeling well," he said as he searched her sunken eyes.

"I'm fine. Exhaustion and cookies."

"In my opinion, cookie indulgence should fix exhaustion," he said on a laugh and walked toward his car as the sun began to streak the sky in brilliant colors.

Within the hour he was behind his desk. He'd stopped by his house, gathered his mail, packed a bag for the weekend, thrown all the presents he had in his car, and changed his clothes.

Now, with a hot cup of coffee rested between his hands, he looked at the logs for the day. Everything was on track for the end of the year, and that was his Christmas bonus to himself, he thought. He'd make the rounds to the sites before heading back to Kelly's and spending Christmas with his family.

Catherine stumbled into his office, a mug of coffee threatening to spill, a pile of paper, her notebook, and a wrapped breakfast sandwich balanced on top.

"Let me help you with that," Ray laughed as he moved around the desk and took the pile from her hands. He laid it on the table and studied her. "Are you okay?"

Catherine let out a ragged breath. "I'm exhausted. Morning sickness isn't just in the morning. No, it gives you reflux, and can keep you up all night. The coffee is decaf. There are no sweeteners or creamers in it, and my doctor told me to stay away from Christmas treats. Are you kidding me?"

Ray didn't mean to laugh, but he did.

Catherine blew a wayward strand of hair from her face and plopped down in one of the chairs at the table. "Sorry. I promise not to be grumpy through my whole pregnancy."

"You forget, I lived with someone who went through this more than once. I can handle it. I'll leave it to Alex to massage your feet and back though."

"Oh, a massage. Doesn't that sound nice?"

He laughed again and retrieved his notes. "But you're doing okay?"

Catherine shrugged as she sipped her coffee and winced at the flavor. "I'm exhausted. Celia Rose has another tooth coming in. Alex was up with her all night. We both have dark circles under our eyes. We look like zombies."

"An extended weekend will do you good."

She nodded. "How's Kelly?" Her lips had turned up into a wide smile.

"She's fine."

"We're closer friends than that, you and me, and me and her. How are things going?"

The smile on his own face couldn't be controlled. "I'm moving back in. I stayed last night because she wasn't feeling very good. The kids said they thought I should just live there. We've had a few very exciting weeks." He could feel the heat in his cheeks.

Catherine shrugged and picked up her notepad. "I've heard," she teased.

Ray figured there were no surprises when it came to what Catherine and Rachel had pulled out of Kelly.

Catherine slipped off her shoes and tucked her feet under her on the chair as she leaned on the table with her elbows, pen in her hand ready to take notes. "Is she feeling better? You said she wasn't feeling good."

"End of semester and every student brought her a plate of cookies. She over-indulged," he said and Catherine nodded slowly. "Besides, like she said, she always gets sick at Christmas. Exhaustion. Treats. Kids bringing germs into the classroom. It's part of the job. But she got sick, and was fine after that." Again the smile crept to his lips, and he knew it said more than it should have.

Still, Catherine studied him.

"What?"

Her eyes went wide, then she picked up her phone and began texting. "Nothing. She's okay to still exchange gifts tonight, right?"

"She's looking forward to it. Be warned that she's bringing plates of cookies. Tell Alex he has to help you with that if you're not supposed to partake."

"Between him and Bruce, I don't see a problem."

When her phone chimed with an incoming text, she grinned. He wondered what she was up to.

CHAPTER 39

$\mathcal{K}$elly pulled up in front of Catherine's house. Lights twinkled from the eaves, and the Christmas tree was prominently displayed in the front window. Snow had come in around lunch time, and now sparkled against the house lights.

The sight was beautiful, and one of the many reasons Kelly loved that time of year. There was a magic in everything—including the cold and snow. The door opened as she started up the walk, and Alex stood there with Celia Rose on his hip.

"Merry Christmas," he said as she approached.

"Merry Christmas. I can't believe how big she is," Kelly said as she passed by them and into the house. "At this age, they grow so fast. It was only a few weeks since I saw her."

"Growth spurt," he teased. "She knows she's going to be a big sister, so she's stepping up. Rachel and Catherine are in the kitchen. My girl and I are headed downstairs to watch TV with Bruce."

He kissed Kelly on the cheek and led the way to the kitchen, where he proceeded to kiss both Rachel and Catherine on the cheeks as well, and then disappeared down the stairs.

"He saw the box under the tree," Catherine said as she set a plate of meats and cheese on the table. "He's like a little kid."

Kelly handed Rachel a plate of cookies, and another to Catherine. "I'm sharing the wealth," she said. "Most years I'm swimming in Starbucks gift cards. This year everyone baked."

Rachel had already retrieved a cookie and had bitten the head off a Santa. "Oh, God! This is fantastic. I'm in heaven. I'll be in a sugar coma by bed time." She took another bite.

Catherine winced. "I'm not ungrateful. Alex and Bruce are going to throw themselves on these," she said. "The doctor cut my sugar intake."

"Well they had to leave my house," Kelly admitted. "I don't care who eats them, or what happens to them. I shared the holiday spirit. Besides, I ate so many last night I was sick."

She noticed Catherine and Rachel exchange looks.

"Ray said you were sick. You're better now?" Catherine asked, offering Kelly a seat and taking one herself.

"Yeah. A moment with my forehead against porcelain, and I was fine," she laughed. "Ray took good care of me." The heat rose in her cheeks and Catherine laughed.

"You know, he blushed when he said that too."

They all laughed, and that fueled Kelly. She'd had close friends, but these two women had become more like sisters in the past few months, and she appreciated that. They could talk about anything, and no one held judgement. She'd always wanted a relationship like that, but she never would have guessed it would come in the way it had.

Rachel leaned her elbows on the table. "Let's get down to business. You're getting back together and it's final, right? Ray told Catherine he was moving home."

Kelly lifted a cookie from the plate Rachel had uncovered, and broke the top off a neon green Christmas tree. "Yes," the word said more than anything else could have.

Both of the women laid a hand on her and encouraged her.

Rachel took another cookie. "I'm so damn happy for the two of you. I know I wasn't around when you were married, but the man never had a bad word to say about you. When he'd talk about you there was a longing. He loved spending time with his kids, and always he had something to add about how you looked or the things you were doing. A jaded ex-husband just didn't act the way that Ray did."

"I'm glad to hear that. We jumped into divorce. I know that now. Hell, I knew it then. But when someone says they want out, you just don't want to hold them back."

"He was stupid," Rachel confirmed as she bit into a cookie that stained her teeth green.

Kelly laughed. "He was stupid. And I was stupid for not fighting for my marriage. I think it'll be different. Besides, I didn't stray even in divorce."

Catherine inched in. "You didn't date or have sex with anyone for all that time?"

"No." She held up a hand. "Well, just prior to Ray coming back into my life in that capacity, I was seeing an old boyfriend from college. We had a few hot nights of kissing, but to be honest, it didn't move me. Ray looks at me and my toes curl, my heart rate kicks up, and everything tingles. Then when he touches me..." again she could feel the heat rise in her cheeks.

Both of the women laughed and Rachel rubbed her belly. "Look at me. I get it. When the man is the right one, you can't keep your hands off him."

Kelly bit the cookie she still held in her hand. "I never stopped loving him. I'm lucky, and I know it. He wants me back and I get to have him back. We'll argue, but I know now we'll work through it. Nothing is ever perfect."

"This is as close as it could possibly be," Catherine confirmed. "I mean you're glowing."

Kelly noticed the two women exchanging glances again.

She brushed the crumbs from her fingers. "I'm happy."

Rachel reached under the table and pulled out a gift bag. She set it on top of the table and grinned. "It's time for presents."

Kelly nodded, and picked up the two bags she had carried in as well.

Catherine rested a hand on Kelly's arm. "You first."

"Okay."

"And listen, I have a gift. I mean like a gift of knowing things."

Rachel nodded. "She looks innocent enough, but she does. She knows things."

"What kind of things?"

"Open the gift," Catherine said as Rachel handed it to her.

Kelly took the bag and lifted the paper off the top. Inside she found bath bombs, facial sheets, nail polish, and chocolates. Just the sight of them made her stomach tighten.

"Keep digging," Catherine instructed.

There were cute socks and a book. She pulled out the book and then studied her two friends.

"*So You're Having Another Baby,*" she read the title and wrinkled up her nose. "I think you gave me the wrong bag."

Catherine shook her head. "Keep digging."

Laying the book on the table, and adding a few of the items to the pile, she dug to the bottom of the bag and retrieved a pregnancy test.

"You guys are serious? You want me to be pregnant so I can go through this with you?" she laughed. "This is a little desperate."

Catherine put her hand on Kelly's arm. "No, I think you should go take the test."

Rachel nodded. "Just do it. She has a gift, and that's it. She just knows. She did the same thing to me. Don't question it."

Catherine bobbed her head in agreement. "Seriously, I knew I was pregnant in a day."

"Not possible," Kelly said.

"Honestly, it's a gift."

"I'm not pregnant." Kelly looked at the test and her stomach knotted. "I'll save this. I mean we've discussed more kids."

"You're going to need it," Catherine said as she broke off a tiny piece of cookie and popped it in her mouth. "I'd say you're about four or five weeks."

"Then I'd already know."

"Would you? I mean you should know," Catherine laughed. "Go take the test."

"I'm not taking this."

Rachel bit into another cookie. "Just go take it. Shut her up," she teased. "Or, give Ray the best Christmas gift ever."

Kelly thought of the previous night. And hadn't she been just a little out of sorts the past week when she woke up?

Of course she had. She'd been out of sorts since the moment Ray kissed her when his father passed away.

Her head was spinning now. Five weeks ago, she and Ray had had their weekend together. She'd lost count of how many times they'd made love that weekend. Since then, well, she wasn't counting that either.

When did she have her last period? She usually kept track of that. Why hadn't she been keeping track of that?

Catherine leaned back in her chair. "You're going pale thinking too hard. Go take the test."

Kelly looked at the box. "I'm not telling either of you what it says," she said as she took the box and headed down the hall to the bathroom.

CHAPTER 40

*K*elly opened the door and the smell of popcorn hit her first. Then her stomach twisted and threatened to retaliate, but she willed it to stay. The kids were in the bath upstairs, and she could hear their little voices. Then she heard Ray's booming voice as he played with them in the water.

Tears welled in her eyes and she pressed her hand to her stomach, which she'd filled with sugary cookies again. Life was perfect just the way it was, wasn't it? The four of them were happy. Everything she'd ever dreamed of was right under that roof.

Ray appeared at the top of the stairs. His shirt was wet, and so was his hair where he'd run his hands through it.

"I thought I heard you. How was your gift exchange?" he asked.

"Good," she heard her voice crack with tears and she swallowed them down. "It was nice."

"You're still not feeling good."

"Let's just say we over indulged in more cookies."

Ray laughed. "If you want, I'll give you a bath when I'm done with these two."

Kelly walked up the steps and he was there to kiss her gently on the lips.

Easing her back he studied her. "Are you okay. Seriously, you don't look well."

"I'm okay," she said as she moved from him and walked toward the bathroom where her children splashed in the tub.

The tears threatened again. These were her loves—her life. With or without Ray, these two people were her everything.

"Mommy, watch my hair," Charlotte demanded as she made her hair stand up to a point.

The joy Charlotte displayed made Kelly laugh, but the tears still threatened.

Connor looked up at her with a watchful eye. "Are you okay, Mom?"

Nothing slipped by them. "I'm just fine sweetheart. I'm going to go change my clothes."

The kids went back to splashing, and when Kelly walked out of the bathroom, she nearly ran right into Ray.

"I started some water for you for tea," he said resting his hands on her arms. "You look like you could use some."

She smiled, drinking in his dark eyes and the feel of his hands on her. She loved him. No matter what, he'd never leave, she knew that now. They were together through the good and the bad, thick and thin, the expected and the unexpected.

"I appreciate that." She took a step, and then retracted. "I love you, Ray. I just want you to know how much I do love you."

He lifted his hand to her cheek and gazed into her eyes. "I love you too, Kel. The hardest part about the past few years, no matter what happened, I always was in love with you. I knew I couldn't move on even if I tried."

KELLY CHANGED INTO HER PAJAMAS, WASHED HER FACE, AND PULLED on a sweater. She walked down to the kitchen and poured herself a cup of hot water and added a tea bag as she heard the stomping of feet running down the stairs.

"Mom, we're going to watch something called *Herbie*," Connor announced from the living room. "Come watch it with us."

Kelly laughed. That had been Ray's favorite movie, and no matter how old or outdated it had become, he never tired of it. Now he shared his joy with their kids.

She blew out a long, steady breath. Catherine and Rachel had gotten her worked up.

Lifting her mug to her lips, she sipped the tea. She needed just a few more minutes to regain her composure. Nothing would change, she thought. Everything would be as perfect as it was in that moment.

RAY TIDIED UP THE LIVING ROOM AND SET THE BOWLS FROM THE popcorn in the sink. He turned out the lights, checked the locks on the doors, and happily walked up the steps, past the photos of his family.

He was sleeping in his home. He was sleeping in his home surrounded by his family. It was forever now.

His heart raced like that of a child who would wake to presents under the tree from Santa. This was his Christmas miracle. This was his shining moment.

Even with the doors closed now, and everyone tucked into bed, he still heard Charlotte talking to her toys. He would remember to cherish every moment of every day from here on out.

Kelly was propped up in bed when he walked into the bedroom. The TV flickered, but she didn't seem to be paying any attention to it.

"I was just thinking how awesome this is," he said and she blinked and looked at him as if she'd only just realized he'd walked into the room.

Ray shut the door behind him and walked toward the bed.

Kelly smiled, but it didn't reach her eyes. "What is awesome?"

Ray pulled back the sheets and climbed in next to her. "That I'm home. I'm here with you in our bed, in our house, with our kids. I can't tell you how many nights I dreamed of this."

Kelly sighed. "Me too."

"I would think you'd be happier."

She bit down on her lip. "I am happy. I am really happy," she said.

"But something is bothering you."

Kelly tucked her lips between her teeth and sat up. She turned to him, so he sat up to meet her. "I'm scared."

That caused him to laugh, though he hadn't meant to. "Why are you scared? We know what we're doing now. There isn't anyone against us. It's you and me and the kids. We're a family again."

"We were a family when we were apart, too."

"Yes, and we worked very hard to make that seamless. Now we know we can work through anything."

Kelly sucked in a deep breath and turned toward him, pulling her legs in and folding them under her. "Something is heavy on my mind. I told you'd I'd never been with anyone else. Since you walked out that door, the only person I was involved with was Jeremy."

He felt a pain in his chest when she mentioned him. "Yeah."

"We kissed—a lot."

"Not something I want to imagine, but okay."

"We never talked about you."

CHAPTER 41

*R*ay's mouth had gone dry. Seriously, what had Rachel and Catherine said to her? What did they even know?

"What about me?" he asked, as he swiveled in the bed to sit across from her just as she was sitting.

"How many women, Ray? How often did you try to forget me or move on from me?"

She was crying now, and he wasn't sure what he was supposed to do with that. Where had all of this come from?

"I thought that was the point, right? You divorce someone and you move on."

"I didn't move on."

"That was your choice, right?" he snapped, but he hadn't meant to. "I mean it wasn't important to you."

"I needed to do what was right for my kids—our kids," she corrected.

"You did. You're an amazing mother, and I'd like to think I'm an amazing father."

Kelly wiped at her tears. "I'm sorry. I'm out of sorts."

"Yes you are, and I'd like to know what's going on."

She shook her head. "Just tell me, Ray. Give me a number so I can move past this."

Ray chewed on his bottom lip and studied her. Craig must have said something to Rachel, who then said something to Kelly to get her so worked up.

"What did Rachel tell you?"

Kelly's eyes grew wide. "She told me nothing. Dear God, how many, Ray? What are you hiding?"

"I'm not hiding anything. I'm just not sure why we're having this conversation. I didn't go behind your back. I didn't cheat on you. We were—are divorced."

Now she sobbed hard, and he wanted to pull her into his arms.

Kelly lowered herself back to the bed and turned from him.

He wasn't going down without a fight. This wasn't going to happen to them.

He laid down behind her and wrapped his arm around her. "Kel, I love you. But I tried like hell to get over you. I messed up our marriage by walking out of it. I take full responsibility for that. And, yeah, I thought it would make me forget, but it didn't. Just the opposite, it made me long for you more."

"I shouldn't have asked. It hurts too much."

Ray rolled her so that she faced him. Brushing away the strands of hair that stuck to her cheeks, he tucked them behind her ear as he searched her eyes. "There were two other women that I spent the night with. Craig and I went out a few times when I was really low, and I ended up going home with someone I picked up."

The disgust that shielded her face was worse than the tears, he decided. "You just picked up women?"

"Two times. But, yeah, for two random nights while we were divorced, I slept with other women. I'm not proud of it. And not that it helps, I was sick after because all I could do was think of you. I felt like I'd cheated on you, and yet again, I mention that we were divorced at the time."

He saw her wince and press her hand to her stomach. Then she jolted from the bed and ran to the bathroom. She slammed the door, and he heard her get sick again.

What was wrong with her? Picking fights and getting sick?

The air left his lungs and he'd remembered her actions nearly seven years ago. The fights she'd start out of nowhere, which included broken glass because she'd thrown a frame at him, and the sickness.

Ray untangled himself from the sheets and ran to the bathroom. He pushed open the door and again found her sitting on the floor, leaning up against the wall.

He took the hand towel, just as he had a few days earlier. He wet it and handed it to her as he sat down on the floor next to her.

"You're picking fights with me," he said softly as he took her hand and laced their fingers together.

"I am."

"You're pretty sick too."

She nodded as she wiped the sweat from her brow. "I am."

Now he felt a lightness in his heart as he lifted her fingers to his lips. "I'll be right back," he said as he stood and left the room.

KELLY CLOSED HER EYES AND WILLED AWAY THE NEXT BOUT OF sickness. Why had she asked him those questions? They'd have talked about it. She had no right to be mad or worked up about it. She was holding her own secrets.

When Ray returned, he sat back down on the floor next to her with a Christmas present in his hands.

"What are you doing?" she asked, finally laughing.

"I was going to give this to you tomorrow night when we opened presents. But I think you need it now."

Ray handed her the box.

Kelly set the towel on the side of the bathtub and began to unwrap the gift. When she opened the box, there was a ring box inside.

Her lip trembled as she lifted the ring box out and looked at Ray.

He took it from her and opened it to reveal a magnificent princess cut diamond setting.

The tears were back, but they didn't hurt this time.

"This is the most unromantic setting," Ray teased. "But I don't want to wait one more second."

He took her hand and slid the ring onto her finger. "Kelly, will you marry me again?"

In the dimly lit bathroom, she nodded, and pulled him to her. "I will marry you, again. I love you. I've never wanted anything so much in my whole life."

Ray eased back and kissed her. "That makes me very happy."

She looked down at the ring. "This is beautiful."

"Not nearly as beautiful as you," he said gazing into her eyes. "Now, my turn. Give me my present—the secret you're keeping from me."

CHAPTER 42

*K*elly's eyes had gone wide. Yeah, she had a secret, he thought, and he knew exactly what it was. Maybe she didn't even know.

"You have something to tell me, right?" his voice shook when he asked.

Kelly stood from her seat on the floor and walked out of the bathroom and out of the bedroom.

Oh, he wasn't just going to let her walk away and ignore him.

When he made it down the stairs, he followed the light to the kitchen where Kelly stood over the gift bag she'd brought home from Catherine's.

"What are you doing?" he asked as she began to pull things from the bag.

"This is the gift I got from Catherine and Rachel," she said as she frantically laid items on the table.

Bath bombs, socks, facial masks, candies. Ray laughed. This is what had her so worked up?

Then she pulled out a book and sat it on the table.

Ray picked it up. *So You're Having Another Baby?*

"Yep. This was my Christmas gift."

He narrowed his eyes on her. "And Catherine and Rachel gave this to you? Why?"

"Because Catherine has this calling. She *just knows things*." She mimicked, he assumed, Rachel and Catherine.

"And what did she know?"

Kelly crossed her arms. "Did you know she was the one that knew Rachel was pregnant? I mean before Rachel knew she was pregnant. She bought Rachel the test."

"I heard something about that." He set the book down. "And why did she give you this book?" His voice was lighter now.

Kelly moved from him and picked up her purse. Again, she rummaged through it and pulled out something. She gripped it in her hand, then held it behind her back.

"Our life is perfect, right?" she asked, again her tone was panicked.

"Absolutely."

"We have two amazing kids."

"We do."

"We're going to get married. We'll all be together..."

"Kelly," he stopped her and grinned. "What does the test say?"

Again, her eyes went wide. When she lifted her hand to hand him what she'd taken from her purse, he noticed she shook.

Ray took the test from her and studied it. There was an ache in his chest when he looked down at it. He'd built the moment in his mind, but now...

"You're not pregnant?" he asked and her eyes grew even wider.

"What?" Kelly pulled the test out of his hand and studied it. "Oh, shit! Wrong one." She dug through her purse and pulled out another. She handed it to him. "There were two tests in the box."

Ray chuckled and looked down at the stick in his hand that distinctly said the word PREGNANT.

. . .

185

KELLY STUDIED HIS REACTION. HIS CHEEKS HAD PINKED. HIS EYES had gone moist. A smile formed on his face that was as wide as she'd ever seen.

When he looked up at her again, he pulled her to him and pressed a hard kiss to her lips.

"We're having a baby," he said and his words were solid and didn't shake.

"It's too soon."

"Too soon for what? We have two kids. We wanted four. This is just what we wanted."

"Years ago."

"Now, Kel. It wasn't right until now."

She studied him. "But we're just getting back together. What are the kids going to think?"

"I don't give a damn what they or anyone else thinks. And it's not like we were strangers. We've been raising our family together this whole time. Honestly, Kel, I'm so happy I could burst."

"You already knew."

"I did," he admitted.

"Did they tell you?"

Ray chuckled. "You told me. You were acting funny."

"What does that mean?"

He caressed her cheek. "Remember how you acted before you knew you were pregnant with Connor, and Charlotte? Actually, now that I think about it, it was worse with Charlotte."

"I was sick and picking fights."

"Right. You threw things at me back then. I think you did better this time," he offered.

"You're happy?"

"Aren't you?"

She nodded and sucked in a breath. "I'm scared to death."

"You've done this before," he reminded her.

"I didn't mean to get pregnant."

"I didn't mean to get you pregnant," he teased and nipped her nose with a kiss. "But here we are. We're having another baby and we're getting married."

"Mommy is having a baby?" Charlotte's tired voice came from the doorway.

Ray pressed his forehead to Kelly's and they laughed. "We need to remember to stay in our room and lock the door if we're going to have important conversations."

Still wrapped in his arms, Kelly turned toward her sleepy children. Charlotte held tight to her unicorn, and Connor held his stuffed bear to his side, as if no one could see it.

"Well, I guess there are no Christmas surprises from us for tomorrow, huh?" Kelly knelt down and opened her arms so that her children would come to her. "I love your daddy very much."

Connor nodded. "We know that."

Kelly held out her hand and showed them the ring. "Daddy gave me this."

Both of the kids looked up at him with furrowed brows. "You said we were going to give it to her together," Connor argued.

"It needed to be given to her tonight. I'm sorry, kiddo."

Kelly turned and looked at him. "They were in on it?"

"On the engagement part. They helped pick it out."

The tears were back, as if a faucet had opened up. Now she remembered that when she was pregnant, she was an emotional mess.

"Why did you give it to her?" Connor asked.

"So that she would tell me her secret," Ray defended.

"What secret?"

"That's she's having a baby," Ray laughed. "Mommy and I are getting married and you guys are getting a baby sister or brother."

Charlotte looked up at him unfazed. "I already knew Mommy was having a baby."

Ray looked at Kelly, and she shook her head. She hadn't told anyone but him. In fact, she had run out of the house and never said another word to Rachel or Catherine either.

Kelly took Charlotte's hands in hers. "How did you know I was having a baby?"

Charlotte shrugged. "Grandpa told me when we went for a walk in my dreams."

The tears came harder now, and Kelly brushed them away with the heel of her hand. "Grandpa told you?"

"He misses us. But he sent us a baby."

Ray knelt down next to Kelly and pulled his children in close, wrapping his other arm around Kelly.

She rested her head to his shoulder. She had nothing to worry about. Everything had just fallen into place.

CHAPTER 43

*I*nstead of a guys' night, New Year's Eve was open to everyone at Toby's house. Charlotte and Connor weren't completely thrilled to be going to their grandmother's for the night, but Uncle Doug had promised that he'd be there and they were staying up until midnight and lighting sparklers.

Ray watched Kelly add a clip to her hair, which she'd piled atop her head in a bun of precise curls.

He moved in behind her and kissed her neck. "The kids just left with my brother, and you look too amazing to take into public. I think we should just stay home and do more of this," he offered as he moved his kisses to her bare shoulder.

"I think we'd better go out while we can," she teased. "I'm older now. I'm not going to bounce back from another baby as easily."

"You're not that old."

"Thank you, but I can tell the difference."

Ray spun her around and risked her lipstick by kissing her deeply, until she wrapped her arms around his neck and took the dive with him. "Let's make a pact that we don't have to stay all night. We can run home at any moment."

189

"That's not going to happen."

"Then let's leave two minutes after midnight so we can get back here and I can spend the first few hours of an amazing new year making love to you, over and over again."

Kelly smiled and pressed a kiss to his lips. "I will absolutely agree to that."

～

THE ENORMOUS HOUSE THAT BACKED UP AGAINST THE FLATIRONS OF Boulder was packed with people. It wasn't only the usual group of friends that gathered, and their wives, whom now had all bonded into sisterhood. Toby had invited everyone he knew, apparently.

When he passed by Kelly and Ray at the door, he had a woman on each arm. Ray had to assume that maybe they were there for show because it wasn't Toby's style to flaunt what he had—including women. In fact, Toby having that many people in one place absolutely didn't make sense to Ray.

"I'm so glad you're here," Toby walked toward them, dropping his arms and the women so that he could hug both of them—or lean on them. "I'm so happy you're here."

Ray placed a hand on Toby's shoulder and eased him back. "You doing okay?"

"Better than okay." He leaned in to Ray's ear to whisper. "I just sold a manufacturing patent for a butt load of money," his breath was hot on Ray's cheek. "I'm rich."

Ray laughed. "You were rich to begin with."

Toby laughed. "I was. I am. But I'm alone," he drew out the word. "I wanna wife."

"Let's talk about that tomorrow."

Toby nodded. "You're getting married," he said leaning closer to Kelly. "He loves you. He always loved you. He was sad without you."

She laughed. "I love him too."

"I have to go mingle. Stay all night, okay?" He stumbled backward, but found his footing and the women he'd discarded.

"I've never seen him like that," Ray said. "Even in college, he was the one who kept his wits about him."

Kelly took Ray's arm. "I remember."

Before they made it into the house a few feet, Craig and Rachel were headed toward them. Craig had his arm wrapped around Rachel's shoulders and her head was down.

"Hey guys," Craig said. "We're headed out."

Ray wondered if the crowd was triggering Rachel's PTSD, but when she lifted her head and sucked in a breath, Ray's sucked in his own breath. "Oh!"

Rachel nodded. "All of a freaking sudden this baby wants to be here. God, I hope he waits." She gripped her stomach.

Ray helped part the people out of their way. "You'll call us?" he called after them.

"We'll call you," Craig shouted back.

As soon as Ray turned back to the room, Kelly pulled him to her. There were tears in her eyes again, but the smile on her face calmed him. "They'll call," he said.

"When they're ready to." She cupped his face in her hands. "I can't believe that'll be us in a few months."

Ray rested a hand on her stomach and smiled. "I'm ready. And I'll be more help than I was before. This is going to be a great year."

ALEX AND CATHERINE WERE IN THE KITCHEN, AND WHEN THEY SAW them walk into the room, Catherine hurried toward Ray and wrapped her arms around him.

"I knew it. I knew it!" She kissed him on the cheek. "I have a gift. I just knew it! Are you happy? Tell me you're happy."

Ray laughed as he kissed Catherine's cheek. "I'm extremely happy—we're extremely happy."

"Can you believe it? We're all having babies this year?" Catherine reached for Alex's hand and he kissed her gently.

Ray couldn't have imagined that in a year with great loss, first Coach, and then his father, that there would be so much happiness too. Rachel and Craig, Alex and Catherine, and of course he had his Kelly back. Yes, he was extremely happy.

HAND IN HAND, RAY WALKED KELLY TO THE GAME ROOM, SO SHE could finally see the room Connor referred to as the *awesome room*.

"What in the hell?" Ray said over the noise and directed Kelly's attention to the corner behind the bar where Bruce was kissing a woman. "Oh, there are going to be fists flying."

"Who is that?" Kelly asked.

"Sarah, Alex's sister."

"Oh!" she said as if she hadn't realized who it was. "And Alex wouldn't approve of that?"

"It's been a running joke since childhood, I guess. Bruce has this underlying crush on Alex's sister. She leads him on, he swoons, and teases that he's going to make a move. Alex threatens to kill him."

"I think that's sweet," Kelly said and Ray turned to look at her, but only noticed Alex and Catherine starting down the stairs.

Ray pulled Kelly toward the bar. Picking up a handful of nuts from the bowl on the bar, he threw them at the back of Bruce's head.

When Bruce lifted his head Ray pointed toward the stairs. In that moment, Sarah scooted out from behind the bar and Bruce wiped his lips with the back of his hand.

"I owe you one," he said as he leaned over the bar.

"What are you doing?"

"Living out a lifelong fantasy," Bruce smiled, and then put his hand on Kelly's arm. "Hey, congrats. I hear you're marrying this slob and having his baby."

"I need to make an honest man of him."

"It's about time someone did." Bruce pulled out a beer and a bottle of water and slid them toward Ray and Kelly. "I'm happy for you both."

WHEN THEY WERE SURE THAT TOBY HAD BEEN TUCKED INTO BED, and Bruce was in charge of making sure everyone left the house in one piece, Ray and Kelly left the party just shy of three o'clock New Year's morning.

"We could watch the sunrise again," Ray offered as they drove toward home.

"I'll see the sun when I open my eyes," Kelly laughed.

"We could drive to Vegas and get married."

She laughed again. "Your mother deserves something to plan for."

"I guess you're right." He was quiet for a moment. "We could go to the hospital and meet Rachel's little girl."

Kelly sighed when he said that. "That would be disrespectful to a new mother. We'll do that tomorrow before the kids are due back."

"It is tomorrow," he teased. "I guess you're going to have to occupy my mind tonight since I must not be ready to go to bed."

Kelly turned her head to gaze at him. "I can keep you occupied."

CHAPTER 44

*K*elly pulled her hair up into a ponytail because she couldn't be bothered to mess with it one more time. She blotted her face with the towel, and took a good look at herself in the mirror.

The blotchy skin, sunken dark eyes, and unruly hair were not making her feel beautiful—though Ray seemed to think she was.

She hadn't been much help over the weekend, moving Ray back into their house. It had been just long enough, she'd forgotten how much pregnancy could wipe away her energy.

"I have to head out in a minute. Are you okay?" Ray stepped into the bathroom behind her and rested his hand on her back.

"I forgot how taxing this is on a body."

"You're doing a great job."

Kelly laughed and turned to fold into his arms. "I know it'll pass."

"Call in a sub."

She shook her head. "I wouldn't do that to my kids or to a sub. I'll be okay. No one at school knows about this yet, so I'll give them a heads up. They'll cover me if I need a break."

Ray kissed her gently on the lips, and it sent a tingle through her body. "I love you, Mrs. Stewart. I'll see you when I get home."

Kelly sighed. "I really like the sound of that, Mr. Stewart."

THE CAR RIDE TO SCHOOL WAS MORE TAXING THAN GETTING READY that morning. Traffic was now backed up. Charlotte and Connor were trying their best to annoy one another, and Kelly wasn't sure she wasn't going to have to pull over and throw up.

That was nerves, she knew. She got them every time they came back from a break. Thankfully, she'd have a few minutes before the kids came into the classroom to calm down. She rubbed her shoulder which had begun to ache, and then turned to tell the kids to pipe down, she wasn't having it this morning.

Ten minutes later they were in the parking lot. She allowed Connor to run around the side of the building to his classroom, and she walked Charlotte to hers, kissing her goodbye before hurrying to her own classroom.

With her bag falling from her shoulder, and the ache becoming sharper, she juggled the bag and unlocked the door.

"Can I help you with that?"

Kelly spun at the voice to find Jeremy standing behind her already reaching for her bag.

"Thank you."

"My pleasure. Can I come in for a moment? I just want to talk. Just for a moment."

Now nerves mixed with the morning sickness that kept threatening her. But she'd give him just a moment.

"Okay," she said pushing open the door.

Jeremy followed as she turned on the lights. He set her bag on her desk, and in a very gentlemanly fashion, folded his hands and stood by the door.

"What did you need to tell me?" Kelly asked as she rubbed her shoulder, and then thought it best to lean against the desk because her knees were wobbly.

"I wanted to apologize for my actions. I shouldn't have gone after Ray the way I did. I think I always knew he'd win you back. He always did." His voice was soft and sincere.

"Thank you."

"I hear that you're engaged and having a baby." That time his voice cracked and it seemed to twist Kelly up.

"Yes. The baby thing was a bit of a surprise."

"They always are," he said stepping closer to her. "I just want the best for you, Kelly. You're always going to be important to me, no matter what."

"I appreciate that," she said as she winced at a pain that shot right through her.

"Is everything okay?"

"It's fine," she growled out as another pain ripped through her causing her to hunch over.

"You're not okay. Let me get you some help."

"No. It'll be…" She sucked in a breath and reached for the desk. Her head was spinning now and the pain that was ripping through her was causing her to see black spots.

The last thing she heard was Jeremy calling her name.

RAY SLAMMED DOWN THE PHONE AND PICKED UP HIS COAT FROM the back of his chair. He'd been in the office less than an hour and there had been nothing but problems. This was what happened when he lost focus.

No, that wasn't fair and he wasn't going to go down that road again. Any lack of focus was his own fault, but this was because of holidays and time off for his crews and vendors, and himself.

He grabbed the file from his desk and headed for the front door. There were some heads that were going to roll, and it was his least favorite thing to do on a Monday morning, or any morning for that matter.

The foreman he'd called in to help him take over the job at hand had pulled up and jumped out of his truck. A delivery truck followed through the gate, and the door to the office opened behind him.

"Ray! Ray!" Catherine called out after him.

"It has to wait, Cathy. I have to go."

"It's Kelly."

"Tell her I'll call her back." He said as he opened the door to his truck and hit the unlock button so the foreman could jump in the other side.

Catherine hurried toward him, her hands on the small swell of her stomach. "Kelly is at the hospital."

The blood drained from his head and the foreman got out of his truck and shut the door.

"Why?"

"I don't know. They just called looking for you. She was just brought in from someone at the school who is there with her now. I don't know anything else. Saint Joe's, go."

He was frozen in place. Every part of him seized up, and he couldn't move.

Immediately his thoughts went to the school and the kids. Rachel had been shot at her school when a student had gone in shooting.

"Where are my kids?"

"I don't know," Catherine said. "I'll find out. We'll make sure they're taken care of. I'll call your mother and brother."

Ray nodded. But he still couldn't move.

"Go," Catherine said stepping to him and kissing his cheek. "We'll take care of everything here."

CHAPTER 45

*R*ay ran into the waiting room at the hospital. Why in the hell was it packed on a Monday morning?

"Kelly Stewart, I'm looking for my wife, Kelly Stewart," he repeated to the woman behind the desk who held up a hand to him.

"Was she brought in by ambulance?"

"I don't know. My wife is here. She's pregnant, and here." His entire body shook. He should have more damn information.

"I brought her," the voice came out of the crowd of people and a moment later Jeremy Cross was standing next to him.

Ray's body went hot, and he grabbed the front of Jeremy's shirt and yanked him in. "What in the hell did you do to her, you son-of-a-bitch!"

The woman behind the desk and two security guards were already headed toward them. One of them grabbed Ray, the other Jeremy.

"I didn't do anything. I was at the school and asked to talk to her. I wanted to wish her well, give my congratulations. That's all. She collapsed right in front of me."

Ray pulled from the security guard and stood in front of Jeremy searching for more.

"Why did she collapse?"

"I don't know. She didn't look good. And then she grabbed her stomach and collapsed. She's in surgery right now." Jeremy moved in and took Ray's shoulders, the security guards standing pressed against them. "I don't know a lot of details. The baby isn't in the right place or something. They have to do surgery because something ruptured. It all happened so fast, Ray, I don't know what happened."

In a moment of weakness, Ray reached for Jeremy and fell against him, his arms wrapped around him. "She can't die."

"They're not going to let that happen, Ray."

RAY PACED IN THE SURGICAL WAITING ROOM ALONE. THEIR FRIENDS had come and they waited downstairs for word. All of them but Rachel who was home with her baby. And just that thought made Ray fall into the chair at his side and sob.

Once they'd figured out who Kelly was and who Ray was, he'd been led to the waiting area and briefed on what was going on.

Kelly's pregnancy had been ectopic, and that too had to be explained.

"The fetus attached in the fallopian tube, and now is causing it to rupture."

It had taken three more rounds of questions from Ray to realize that the baby had been lost.

He buried his face in his hands, his elbows rested on his knees. Kelly was safe, he reminded himself. They'd gotten her into surgery before it had become life threatening. Jeremy had saved her life, and at some point he'd have to thank him for that.

It was okay, he kept telling himself. They were all together again, and they'd get through it. Charlotte and Connor would grow to understand—he'd grow to understand. Ray would take care of Kelly forever and help her through this devastating loss. The important thing was they were a family, and families endured pain and heartache. They'd already told him that she could still have more children. This wasn't anyone's fault, it just happened.

But if they never had any more children, it was okay. They had each other and they had Connor and Charlotte.

"Are you doing okay?" Rachel's voice broke through his silent sobbing. He lifted his head and stood, pulling her to him.

"What are you doing here?"

"I'm a licensed therapist here to help you through your grieving," she said matter-of-factly. "How are you?"

He eased back, keeping her hands in his. "Confused. Mad. Miserable. Scared. Mad," he said again.

"That's good."

"Good."

Rachel nodded. "You're identifying very well, and those are all valid feelings."

She moved to sit down, easing him down next to her. "Have you talked to Kelly yet?"

"She's still in surgery. They thought she'd be out in a few minutes, but then I have to wait to see her in recovery."

"Someone is getting the kids?"

Ray wiped his hand across his nose and sniffed back tears. "My mother and brother are picking them up. The school knows what's going on. She was there when it happened."

"Good, someone was around when it happened. I know it can come on suddenly."

Ray fisted his hand. "Jeremy Cross was with her when it happened."

"Oh," Rachel drew out the word. "Why?"

"He'd stopped in to congratulate her on the baby and the engagement. I hate to say he was being an upstanding human being."

"We can see it as a blessing. He was there."

Ray let out a ragged breath. "Yeah, he was there. I'll thank him for that someday."

When the surgeon walked in, they both stood. "She's out of surgery and has been moved to recovery. I want to let you know I'm very sorry for your loss. These kinds of pregnancies are rare, but they happen."

Ray wiped his eyes. "She's okay?"

"We removed the one fallopian tube. There was no damage to the ovary or the uterus. And we were able to save the other tube. If she wants to, she should be able to have more children. And, since she's gone through this, they'll watch for it again."

"Thank you," Ray said, still holding tightly to Rachel.

"They'll come for you when you can go back."

The surgeon left the room, and Rachel wrapped her arms around him again. "I'm going to go down and let them know what's going on. Everyone is still down there."

Ray chuckled. "They can go home."

"You can say that, but those are your brothers—your family. They'll be there for you, Ray, no matter what you're going through."

"I can never thank everyone enough for what they do for me. And here you are when you should be home with your daughter."

"Angela will understand," she said with a wide smile. "Remember, she's already gone through trauma too and fought through it," Rachel referred to her shooting when she wasn't much further along than Kelly had been. "You let us know what we can do for you, Ray. You're our family. We take care of family."

He pulled her in one more time and kissed her cheek as the nurse walked into the room.

"You can see her now."

201

*K*elly's eyes were closed when Ray walked into the room. Her skin was pale and her hair a mess on the pillow behind her.

An IV was attached to her arm, and there was a sensor on her finger. She'd had two babies, but that was the only time Ray had ever seen her in the hospital. She wasn't sick, usually. She'd never been in an accident. She'd never needed surgery.

Her eyes opened slowly. "Hey," she said with gravel in her voice.

"Hey." His feet seemed stuck in place, but with some thought, he was able to move them. He took her hand and willed away the tears, but they broke through anyway. "I love you, Kel."

She nodded slowly. "Still?"

"Forever. Nothing is going to take that away."

Her lip trembled. "I lost the baby."

"No, the baby was lost. You didn't do that. It just happened."

She nodded again as if she understood he didn't blame her. "Tell me what they did."

Ray pulled up the chair next to the bed and sat down. He

relayed the same information that the doctor had given him and Kelly nodded her head as she took in the information.

"Who has the kids?" she finally asked.

"My mom. She's picking them up from school. She's only going to tell them that you got sick. I'll talk to them when I get them home. They're going to want to keep you for the night."

Her eyes grew heavy. "Jeremy has my ring," she said before she drifted to sleep again.

Ray drew in a deep breath. Well, it looked as if he was going to have that conversation with the man sooner than later.

RAY HAD STAYED AT THE HOSPITAL UNTIL SEVEN O'CLOCK, AND then he figured he'd better get the kids and have that talk.

As he drove away he called Catherine and had her fill him in on everything that had happened at the office, which she'd gotten from the foreman. He knew she'd spent the better part of the day at the hospital, but she'd been working as she'd waited for information.

Instead of driving to his mother's house first, Ray detoured to Jeremy's. The Christmas tree still shimmered in the window, and Ray noticed the TV was on and the kids were there. God how he wished it hadn't been Jeremy's week to have the kids. He didn't want to have any kind of conversation in front of them.

When Ray reached the front door, it opened without him knocking, and Jeremy stepped out into the dark cold and closed the door behind him.

"I assume you came for this," Jeremy said holding out the ring Ray had slipped onto Kelly's finger. "It's beautiful."

"Thank you."

"I forgot it was in my pocket at the hospital," Jeremy admitted. "Things were a little—heated."

"I'm sorry for that."

"Don't be. I deserved it after what I did to you. We've decided it's best to pull our kids out of the school, just so you know. My ex isn't too keen on me having them there knowing my past with Kelly."

"I'm sorry to hear that, for the kids' sake. It's a good school. But I can't say I blame your ex for her thoughts on that."

"Kelly's okay?"

"She's still in the hospital for the night."

"Ray, I'm really sorry about the baby. I understand that kind of loss. We went through it twice before Sammy was born. Just know that you never forget it, the baby will stay in your heart, but you will both go on."

Ray batted his eyes as they grew damp. He wouldn't have imagined it would be Jeremy that brought some peace to the situation.

He looked down at the ring. "I assume she's going to fight me over this a little, getting married again and moving on. You know, anger is part of the mourning and healing process. I just have to be the bigger person and remember not to walk away this time."

"Don't let her go, Ray. She's too damn special and you love her too damn much."

~

THE KIDS ASKED EVERY QUESTION THEY COULD IN THE CAR.

"Where is Mommy?"

"Why did Mommy get sick?"

"When do we get to see our baby?"

"Did Mommy have the baby?"

"Can we get McDonalds and then go see Mommy?"

Ray gripped the steering wheel as he pulled the van into the driveway and put it in park.

"We're going to go inside and get our baths since Grandma

fed you dinner. Then I will talk to you about what happened to Mommy."

They both went quiet as they gathered their things and climbed out of the van.

There was little commotion as they climbed up the stairs and got ready for the bath that Ray drew for them.

As he soaped up their hair, he noticed their eyes turned toward him. "Okay, guys, the reason your Mommy got sick was because the baby was growing in the wrong place," he said leaning his forearms on the bathtub. How the hell did you explain something like this to a six-year-old and a four-year-old?

"Where is the baby now?" Connor asked, and Ray was grateful. For some reason, he thought the answer he would come up with for that was easier.

"The baby went to live with Grandpa in heaven," he said and he watched both sets of eyes grow damp.

"I want to see the baby," Charlotte said.

"We can't. All we can do is pray that the baby is safe and happy in heaven."

The tears fell from Charlotte's eyes. "Maybe Grandpa will show me the baby in my dreams, like he did before."

Now Ray cried, but he nodded. "Yeah, sweetheart. Maybe he will. And if he does, you tell the baby that Daddy and Mommy love him, or her. Okay?"

Charlotte nodded as she wiped her tears and Connor put a hand on her shoulder to comfort her.

CHARLOTTE FELL ASLEEP THE MOMENT HER HEAD HIT THE PILLOW, though she'd needed a lot more kisses and a few more stuffed animals surrounding her.

When Ray went to Connor's room, he was wearing the jersey his Uncle Doug had bought for him. "Is Mommy sad?"

Ray sat down on the bed next to his son. "She's very sad."

"Is she disappointed that she only has me and Charlotte?"

Ray brushed the blond hair from his son's forehead. "Oh, no. The first thing she did was ask about you two. Your mommy loves you so much. She was excited to share the baby with you, not to replace you. And she's going to need all your special love now, more than ever."

Connor nodded. "Do I get to see her tomorrow?"

"She should be home when you get home from school."

"Do we have to go to school?"

Ray smiled and kissed the top of Connor's head. "Yes you do, so get some sleep."

CHAPTER 47

*K*elly had cried from the time they'd left the hospital until she tucked herself into her bed before noon. Ray found that anything he said to her caused her to cry, but he had to keep her talking to him, she had to know it was time to heal.

The drapes and blinds had been closed in the bedroom, but when he opened the bedroom door, she hadn't moved from where she'd bundled herself under the covers.

"I brought you some lunch," he said carrying in the plate he'd filled.

"I'm not hungry."

"I'm sure you're not, but you need food to keep your strength up to heal."

Now she rolled onto her back. "What's the use?"

He had to remind himself that the feelings she was having were valid, even if they were grim.

Ray sat down on the edge of the bed, setting the plate on the nightstand. "I know you're miserable right now. You deserve to be. But the kids need you, and you need them. They'll be home in a few hours, and they're very anxious to see you."

"I'm going to break down."

"So do that with them. We all need to mourn this. Kelly, we lost our baby. They lost a sibling. If things had gone wrong, we would have lost you too. But we didn't. So we need to pull together and heal as a family."

She sat up and now wrapped her arms around him. "I was scared, Ray. I was so scared."

He felt her tremble. "I have you, baby," he whispered in her ear as he held her. "I have you."

She sobbed against him, and he held her for hours. What else could he do? They'd lost so much, just when they'd found each other again. Well even this wouldn't tear them apart, he promised her and himself. For better or worse, in sickness and in health, only death would part them from there on.

Ray had convinced her to eat when he went to pick up the kids from school. He took time to go into the office and explain the situation. Women that Kelly worked with began to cry and hugged him tightly, sharing the caring words for her and their condolences.

The kids sat quietly in the car on the ride home. Ray had been prepared for a million questions, but they had none. Charlotte's only request was to stop and buy Kelly flowers. They did just that.

When they walked into the house, Ray was happy to find Kelly seated on the couch, her feet propped up on the coffee table. She'd managed to change her clothes, and he wondered how much that had hurt her. Her hair was brushed and pulled into a ponytail high on her head, and he noticed she'd even added mascara and a bit of lipstick. It made her look as if she felt a little better, but he was sure it was all an act to ease the kids around her.

On her stomach she held a pillow to her, and he knew that was to protect her.

Charlotte ran to her, handed her the flowers, and curled up next to her. She began to cry the moment Kelly wrapped her arm around her. Connor stood just outside of the living room and watched his sister cry in his mother's arms. Ray wrapped an arm around his shoulders.

"You should go talk to her," he said, but Connor clung to his side.

"I don't want to hurt her," he whispered.

"C'mon. I'll go with you."

Ray led the way and Connor followed close behind. Sitting next to Kelly, Ray took her hand, kissed her fingers, and interlocked their fingers. With his other arm, he pulled Connor onto his lap.

Connor clung to the little bear they had purchased at the store with the flowers. He looked at it and then handed it to Kelly.

"I thought this would make you happy," he said as Kelly let go of Ray's hand and took the bear. "You could hold it like you would have the baby."

"Thank you, honey," she said holding the bear to her chest. "I love him." She reached for Connor's hand and held it, while he sat on his father's lap. "I love you all. You know that, right?"

They all nodded their heads.

"Are you okay?" Connor asked. His voice was soft.

"I'm okay," she assured him, giving his little hand a squeeze.

"And the baby went to live with Grandpa in heaven?"

Kelly exchanged glances with Ray, and he knew she was grateful that that was what he'd told them. They seemed to understand it all in those terms.

"Yes, sweetheart. The baby went to live with Grandpa in heaven. So someday, we'll all get to meet. But for now, Grandpa and the baby will watch over us and make sure we're safe here —together."

Charlotte wiped her wet eyes, and wrapped her arms around Kelly's neck. "You promise that you'll get married still and Daddy can stay here forever?"

"I need that now more than ever. I want us all together, baby. We need to be together. I love Daddy, so much."

Ray reached for her hand again. "Maybe what we need to do is plan a wedding. The four of us. We'll invite our friends and the grandparents, but the four of us will plan it. We'll make sure to do something very special that we can include the baby somehow too. What do you think?"

Connor turned on his lap. "You mean I can help you?"

"That's what I mean. Maybe you'll be my best man too?"

"What does that mean?"

"It means you'll stand with me when I marry Mommy. You'll hand me the ring. It's a pretty grown up job, but I think you can handle it."

Connor nodded. "I want to do that."

Charlotte wiped the last of her tears. "Can I be a flower girl?"

Kelly kissed Charlotte's cheek. "Is that what you want?"

"Yeah. I want a pretty dress and flowers."

Kelly laughed, and it warmed Ray to his core. They were going to survive this. They were going to move on together—as a family.

EPILOGUE

*C*harlotte held her basket of rose petals, with the stuffed bear, and her mother's hand as they walked toward Ray and Connor.

Surrounded by their friends and family, on a red clay trail in Red Rocks park on the cool March Saturday, Kelly walked toward the only man she'd ever loved. She understood blessings more now, and Ray Stewart, and their children, were hers.

When they reached Ray, he pulled her to him pressing a kiss to her lips and she laughed. "You're supposed to wait until the minister says you can kiss me."

"I couldn't wait," he said. "Do you have any idea just how beautiful you look?"

"Do I look beautiful, Daddy?" Charlotte tugged on Ray's jacket.

He picked her up and placed her on his hip. "So beautiful," he said kissing her on the nose and then set her down next to Connor, who tugged her next to him.

Kelly listened as the minister talked about love and commitment to one another—and she was ready. He talked about love and loss, and Kelly looked down at her children who stood shoulder to shoulder.

When they turned to say their vows, Ray's eyes were filled with tears, and she batted away the tears that pooled in her eyes.

"I remember the first time I saw you," Ray began. "You were sitting on campus, on the lawn. Your hair was over your shoulder. There was an enormous book of psychology on your lap, and you looked up at me. In that moment a spark lit in my heart and I knew you were the woman I was going to marry. How could I have ever known we'd take this adventure twice and have these two amazing kids to show for it."

There was a twisting in her stomach, and she knew that was the memory of the baby that didn't join them. But even in their love, they'd created the baby.

"I'll love you forever, Kel. I'll fight like hell to keep you. From the moment I met you I wanted you as my wife, and that hasn't changed."

Kelly wiped away the tears that had escaped. She scanned a look out at their friends. Rachel held her daughter and Craig's arm draped over her shoulders. They'd endured trauma to stand there as a family.

Alex held Celia Rose on his hip and Catherine rested her hands on her enlarged belly. They had taken a leap of faith when they found out about Celia Rose, and now they were having another baby. They understood the meaning of family.

Bruce wrapped his arm around Sarah, who rested her head on his shoulder. There was a spark there, amidst a friendship. But didn't every good love story start with a friendship, she thought?

And Toby, with his hands folded in front of him watched them with a smile. Sometimes comfort in life came from knowing exactly who you were.

Charlotte petted the stuffed bear that she carried in her basket, and Connor kicked a pebble at his feet.

She and Ray shared all of this, and they would forever.

"After our first date you said to me, *don't make plans for the next sixty years.*" Ray chuckled as she recalled that conversation. "My schedule is wide open. I'll spend it with you watching our children grow into well-adjusted adults and have families of their own. I'll spend it with you traveling this world. I'll spend it with you on the court with your friends, who are your family, and listening to you laugh and enjoy this very life we share. I'm here for you always, Ray, for the next sixty years, until forever. I love you."

Ray kissed her again, lingering as everyone watched.

"I take you again as my wife, Kelly. To have and to hold forever."

"And I take you, Ray, again, as my husband. To have and to hold forever."

It was then that the minister took over the ceremony and introduced them as husband and wife, again.

Amongst the cheers, Ray planted a kiss on her lips that had her dizzy. It would always be like that, she thought. It always had been. When he eased from her, he picked up Charlotte, and then Connor, and the four of them wrapped their arms around each other.

Something had been found that day that Ray accidentally kissed her in the parking lot, and it was a glorious feeling to be a family again.

SOMETHING FORBIDDEN

We hope you enjoyed book one in the Funerals and Weddings
Series, *Something Found.*
Please enjoy an excerpt from book four,
Something Forbidden.

FUNERALS AND WEDDINGS SERIES, BOOK 4

Sometimes you have
to break a promise
to find new love.

Something
FORBIDDEN

BERNADETTE MARIE
BESTSELLING AUTHOR OF THE DEVEREAUX FAMILY SERIES

SOMETHING FORBIDDEN

Noises from upstairs had Sarah staring at the ceiling. Her head pounded from the amount of wine she'd had to drink at Kelly and Ray's wedding, and the lack of sleep she'd gotten after that.

An arm was draped over her, and there was a soft snore coming from the man next to her. She turned her head to see Bruce with a content smile, even in sleep. What in the hell had they done?

Oh, she knew what she'd done. She'd played out that scenario in her head a million and one times since she was a teenager. But, God, she wasn't a teenager anymore. Bruce was her brother's best friend. She'd known the man, whose bare leg brushed up against hers, since she was five.

And since she was five, her brother Alex had warned her to stay away from Bruce, and vice versa. Well, she could officially say that neither of them had heeded the warnings, and now here they were—naked, and in the basement apartment of her brother's house.

"You are thinking way too hard when you should be sleeping," Bruce's voice broke through the silence, though only a whisper dipped in sleep.

"They're up," she whispered. "We were going to be out of here before they got up."

"It's five-thirty in the morning. They have an infant. It always sounds like that up there."

Sarah rolled toward him. "How in the hell are we going to get me out of here?"

"Wait until you hear running water, then you'll know they're in the shower."

She snorted a quiet laugh. "They shower together? One of them will be up."

He shook his head, rustling his mussed hair against the pillow. "They do, in fact, shower together. It saves time and money, he says. They can also put the baby in her seat while they shower real fast, and sometimes they take her in with them so they don't have to do the whole bath thing."

"You have a lot of information."

"These walls aren't as thick as they should be. But it's freaking cheap to live here, so here I am. Besides, they'll leave early for basketball at the Y. They stop for donuts on Sundays."

She'd lost track of the day, she decided, and let her body relax against the bed.

"I play with you guys every week. I never get donuts."

Bruce chuckled. "I'll get you donuts. I'll get you anything you could ever want."

"I want him not to kill us."

Bruce shrugged.

Yeah, they were screwed.

The timing of all of this sucked. Sarah had moved back home with her mother while her new townhouse was being built. She wasn't in any better a situation than Bruce was. She might not be a teenager anymore, but she was going to have to sneak around like one if she was going to enjoy his company.

So, there they would hide, in Bruce's basement apartment

with her brother living his life upstairs with his wife and daughter.

"Why didn't you move into Catherine's place when she moved in here?" she whispered, which she'd been doing all night.

"Too much money. Remember, I was broke and desolate when I moved in here when Craig owned it. Things have only slightly gotten better in the financial department."

"Toby doesn't pay you well?" She teased, referring to the job another one of his best friends had given him in his high tech business.

He chuckled softly. "I'm paid well. But I have to build a nest egg back up to get on my feet."

Okay, she understood that, but at that moment she wished he'd moved into Catherine's old place.

"He's going to kill us," she said and Bruce tightened his arm around her.

"It would be totally worth it," he grinned again, his eyes still closed.

"We're going to have to talk about this."

"I'm sure we will."

"You're not taking this very seriously, are you?"

His eyes opened slowly. "Sweetheart, you have no idea how seriously I'm taking this. I'm enjoying every single second of you being right here. Let me enjoy it."

Footsteps above them had her gripping the sheet around her. God, why hadn't they gone to a hotel? Because all of her money was tied up in her new house and Bruce was a bit down on his luck, as he'd reminded her.

Not that there would ever be a good time for them to be together, but now certainly wasn't it.

Everything between them had changed on New Year's Eve thanks to a little too much alcohol.

Since they'd been teenagers, they'd flirted, and tossed it around in front of Alex to make him mad. But they both understood the situation. Anything between them was forbidden, because Alex said so.

Then again, who the hell was he to say they couldn't be together?

On New Year's Eve, they'd consumed enough alcohol, and mixed among the crowd, in Toby's enormous house, and they'd kissed. Years and years of pent up lust had broken free that night.

Thinking about that kiss still made her insides sizzle. Who knows where it might have ended had Ray not stopped them before Alex walked into the room?

Now, one wedding reception and plied with more alcohol, look where they'd landed.

Bruce's hand slid under the sheet and over her stomach. "You're thinking too much again."

"I can't help it."

"He never comes down here. Don't worry."

"I am worried."

"I know. So you'd better be very quiet," he said as he rolled himself on top of her.

"Not now that they're awake," she argued. Even as she did, she wrapped her arms around his neck.

"They were awake last night, too. We were just very quiet."

"He's going to kill us," she repeated.

Bruce lowered his mouth to hers. "No, he's only going to kill me. But we'll see how long we can go until he does."

When he kissed her, all of the common sense fell out of her head, again. She'd been chasing this moment all her life. There hadn't been a day that she hadn't had a crush on Bruce Griffin, but she'd known all along nothing would come of it.

PLEASE REVIEW

We hope you enjoyed Something Found by Bernadette Marie. If you did, we would ask that you please rate and review this title. Every review helps our authors.

Rate and Review: Something Found

5 Prince Publishing
Arvada, Colorado, USA

MEET THE AUTHOR

Bestselling Author Bernadette Marie is known for building families readers want to be part of. Her series The Keller Family has graced bestseller charts since its release in 2011. Since then she has authored and published over forty-five books. The married mother of five sons promises romances with a Happily Ever After always... and says she can write it because she lives it.

Obsessed with the art of writing and the business of publishing, chronic entrepreneur Bernadette Marie established her own publishing house, 5 Prince Publishing, in 2011 to bring her own work to market as well as offer an opportunity for fresh voices in fiction to find a home as well.

When not immersed in the writing/publishing world, Bernadette Marie can be found spending time with her family, traveling, and running multiple businesses. An avid martial artist, Bernadette Marie is a second degree black belt in Tang Soo Do, and loves Tai Chi. She is a retired hockey mom, a lover of a good stout craft beer, and might have an unhealthy addiction to chocolate.

OTHER TITLES FROM

5 PRINCE PUBLISHING

www.ingramcontent.com/pod-product-compliance
Lightning Source LLC
Chambersburg PA
CBHW030515020726
47494CB00004B/1099